THE ETHICAL EQUATIONS ... The first contact in deep space with an alien spaceship ...

INTERFERENCE ... Buck's job was investigation and cure of television interference sources – but this source was rather difficult to attack ...

DE PROFUNDIS ... Monsters called Shadi, who live in the deepest caves, armed with tentacles and eighty eyes ... and the tale of one who got away ...

PIPELINE TO PLUTO ... Freight was put in the Pipeline's ships on Earth and practically simultaneously freight was taken out on Pluto. But it didn't make an instantaneous trip ...

SCRIMSHAW ... The old man just wanted to get back his memory – and the methods he used were gently hellish ...

IF YOU WERE A MOKLIN ... Those that live near the forest are greenish, and have saucer eyes, and their noses can wriggle like an Earth rabbit – above all Moklins *love* humans ...

Edited by Brian Davis

The Best of Murray Leinster

CORGI BOOKS
A DIVISION OF TRANSWORLD PUBLISHERS LTD

THE BEST OF MURRAY LEINSTER

A CORGI BOOK 0 552 10333 0

First publication in Great Britain

PRINTING HISTORY
Corgi edition published 1976

Acknowledgements
Time to Die: Astounding Science Fiction, January 1947
The Ethical Equations: Astounding Science Fiction, June 1945
Symbiosis: Collier's, January 1947
Interference; Astounding Science Fiction, October 1945
De profundis; Thrilling Wonder Stories, Winter 1945
Pipeline to Pluto: Astounding Science Fiction, August 1945
Sam, this is you: Galaxy, March 1955
The Devil of East Lupton: Thrilling Wonder Stories, August 1948
Scrimshaw: Astounding Science Fiction, February 1956
If you was a Moklin: Galaxy, September 1951

Corgi Books are published by
Transworld Publishers Ltd,
Century House, 61–63 Uxbridge Road,
Ealing, London W5 5SA
Made and printed in Great Britain by
Cox & Wyman Ltd., London, Reading and Fakenham

INTRODUCTION

WILLIAM FITZGERALD JENKINS was born in Norfolk, Virginia, on the 16th of June, 1896; he died almost exactly 79 years later, on the 8th of June, 1975. In between these two dates he had given nearly fifty years of entertainment to science-fiction readers under his better-known *alter ego* – Murray Leinster.

Leinster never meant to become an author – SF or otherwise: his early ambition was to become a scientist. That this would not have been an impossible dream is shown by the fact that his very last appearance in an SF magazine* was as author of an article on his own invention – Jenkins Systems. The Front-Projection backdrop technique is now an accepted part of the television and film-making industries and it is salutary to remember that (as with Arthur Clarke and the communication satellite) the process was pioneered by a science-fiction writer.

But Murray Leinster became a writer, not a scientist; he was an established free-lance author by the time he was 21 having in the process 'starved to death only twice'. His first out-and-out SF piece, 'The Runaway Skyscraper' appeared in the February, 1919, issue of *Argosy*: it was so well received by its readers that Leinster remained faithful to that periodical until Vol. 1, No. 1 of a certain *Astounding Stories* tempted him into the SF magazine field with a short story: 'Tanks'. Subsequently Leinster produced a great deal of SF with much of it – perhaps some of the best – appearing in that same magazine, still going strong as *Analog*.

Although writing predominantly for the pulp or semi-pulp market, Leinster always credited his readers with intelligence; he never wrote down to his audience, he never failed to keep abreast of the latest developments. Perhaps that is why, at the

* 'Applied Science Fiction.' *Analog*, November, 1967.

age of 66, he was voted one of six favourite *modern* writers of SF. The following year (1963) he was Guest of Honour at the 21st World Science-Fiction Convention in Washington.

A relatively small part of Murray Leinster's total output was in the field of SF. Nevertheless his stories in this field are easily the best remembered. This collection brings together a selection of some of his lesser-known SF work, written in the decade immediately following the end of the Second World War. Together they demonstrate the talent that made Murray Leinster so deservedly popular.

BRIAN DAVIES

TABLE OF CONTENTS

TIME TO DIE

Crime. Leinster was a very moral writer. Almost without exception virtue received its just – if delayed – reward, and the nasties received their come-uppance. Occasionally the innocent suffered (especially in the earlier pre-war universal-catastrophe novels), but generally speaking when someone died you know he deserved it. Sometimes, however, even the villain got a second chance; what he did with it – well, that's something else again.

RODNEY sat on the cot in his cell and stared at a white-hot splash of sunlight shining straight down on the stone floor between the death cells. He was literally dazed. But gradually the news his lawyers had sent him fought itself to the status of a fact. There would be no second reprieve. There would be no commutation. In spite of his standing as having one of the four best brains in the country, in spite of his reputation as possibly the most competent physicist alive, he was going to be executed like a common felon for a commonplace murder. His lawyers could do no more. In exactly three days, prison guards would come and shave his head and slit his trouser legs, and then march him down the corridor to the little green door at its end, and they would take him through it into a room in which there was a squat and ugly and quite horrible chair. They would strap him in that chair and put wetted electrodes to his flesh, and a white-faced man would throw a switch, and Rodney's body, already dead, would struggle convulsively against its doom—

He cracked, suddenly. His flesh crawled as if every separate cell of his body raised a frightened clamor against its coming dissolution. His bones turned to water. His throat was suddenly dusty-dry. He found his hands clawing aimlessly. He heard himself making noises. They were partly gasps and partly sobs and partly self-stifled screams of terror.

He heard the sounds, and he felt contempt for himself. But he could not stop. His body made shaking, convulsive movements. Great tears poured from his wide-opened eyes, empty of everything but pure animal panic. The noises grew louder. Presently he would be screaming. And, if the doctor did not come in time; if somehow he could conceal his state until no dosage of drugs could ease it, he would be quite mad and then they would not execute him. He would live—

Then there was a noise somewhere close by. It was merely the creaking of springs on the cot in the other death cell, now inhabited by one Limpy Gossett. But Limpy was listening. He was a murderer, too. He had been condemned a second time for his second murder. He was to follow Rodney through the door at the end of the corridor. They had talked often, in the past few weeks, and Rodney felt an illimitable contempt for his fellow criminal. But pride forbade that he let Limpy hear him.

Limpy's voice came, reverberating endlessly against the stone walls and iron bars and iron rafters and roof of the deathhouse.

'It got you, guy?'

Rodney would have welcomed madness, because it would have kept his body alive. But Limpy was a mere professional criminal. His two murders had been incidental to his profession of burglary. His brain hardly rated above a moron's classification. So Rodney clamped his lips shut and fought desperately for composure. After seconds he said, as if drowsily:

'What's that? Limpy, did you say something?'

'Yeah,' said the reverberating voice. Limpy was invisible. Rodney had never seen him. But his voice was deep bass, and the echoes in the deathhouse gave it an awesome quality which no amount of bad grammar could quite take away. 'I asked did it get you. I heard you makin' noises.'

Rodney stirred on his cot. He feigned a yawn.

'I had a nightmare,' he said. 'A cyclotron sprouted arms and legs and went racing through the lab—'

His own voice echoed, but it would not have the quality of Limpy's. He waited, his hands clenched.

'Too bad,' rumbled the unseen Limpy. 'You only got three days, guy. Three days an' they march you through the little green door. I got somethin' to tell you when you crack up. It'll help. Let go, fella. What you hangin' on for?'

'Why should I crack up?' demanded Rodney.

'Because,' said the booming voice, 'you got a chance then. I get one too – maybe. There's a trick y'can work. I can't, but I seen it work once. If I seen it again, maybe I'd get the trick of it.'

Rodney, wetting his lips, said skeptically:

'Escape, eh?'

'Yeah,' said the invisible voice. 'From the deathhouse. I seen a fella named Fellenden do it. Ever hear of him?'

'Not likely,' said Rodney. He despised Limpy and all he stood for. He, Rodney, was another order of human being entirely. He— But then he said sharply: 'Fellenden? You mean the chap who worked out the indeterminacy field for electron telescopes?'

Silence, as if the unseen Limpy had shrugged. But his bass voice, echoing, said:

'I wouldn't know. He bumped his wife. He was gonna get the hot seat. We was in the deathhouse at Joliet together. He got away. Skipped. Blew. They never knew how he done it. *I* couldn't. But I got a commutation later on, an' after, I got out. Remember him?'

Rodney said suddenly:

'That's right! Fellenden did kill his wife! He left a lot of work undone, and some of it nobody could quite carry on—'

'O.K.,' said the rumbling voice. 'That's the guy, I guess. We used to talk, same as you an' me. He was workin' on a idea to get away. He told me. "Helped to talk things out," he said. It was a trick to get away clean. When you crack up, maybe you can do it, an' maybe you can explain it to me first. Let go, fella!'

The patch of sunlight shone white-hot. For an hour every

day it shone into the deathhouse. Its reflection was a soft bright glow which should have been beautiful – but there can be no beauty in twin rows of death cells.

Rodney swallowed. His throat was still dry.

'Why wait?' he asked, with an effect of cynicism. 'If it needs desperation, I'm all set now! What've I got to lose beyond a couple of days of waiting?'

His voice sounded all right, but he was shaking all over. He stared through tool-steel bars across the corridor with its spot of sunshine, and into the depths of another cell just like his own, but untenanted.

'Fellenden said,' said Limpy, 'that a fella hangin' on couldn't work it. A guy's got to use all his brains. If he's defiant, an' clingin' to excuses for what he done, an' insistin' he hadda right to or hangin' on to hope, that's part of his brain that won't work free. A fella's got to be cracked up or else plenty sorry so he don't care what part of his brain gets stirred up.'

Rodney said skeptically:

'Ah! No suppressions. No memory blocks. If that means no inhibitions, I qualify! But what's this, Limpy? Self-hypnosis?'

Limpy's voice rolled, and yet was casual.

'He called it time-travelin'.'

Rodney stiffened. But that was nonsense! Fellenden hadn't accomplished time travel! He'd devised a field of quite ridiculous simplicity which eliminated the indeterminacy factor that had made electron telescopes impossible. There would be no electron telescopes but for Fellenden. It was true that there was still controversy over how his field worked. Nobody knew what his theory had been. It was known only that the field worked. But time travel—

'That's crazy,' jeered Rodney. 'How'd he do it? But it's impossible!'

Again there was a pause as if Limpy shrugged.

'He said we do it all the time. We used to be in yesterday. After a while we'll be in tomorrow. Like bein' on a train that a while back was in a jerkwater town named Tuesday, an'll reach a town named Wednesday presently. That's time travel!'

Rodney laughed shortly, but with a catch in his breath.

'Tell me about his escape,' he commanded.

Limpy's voice rolled in every crack and cranny of the death-house. After every word there was a whispering echo that lingered with a queerly solemn persistency.

'The night he left,' the voice said quietly, 'he grinned at the guard when he was makin' last inspection. "I'm escapin' to-night Clancy," he says. An' the guard says, "Says you!" An' Fellenden says, "That's right. Better tell the warden, or you'll catch hell when I turn up missin'." Clancy did. That guy Fellenden was smart. They knew it. They come an' turned his cell inside out. They stripped him an' hunted over that place like nobody's business. They didn't find anything. Natural! An' Fellenden says, "I'm glad you did this, Warden. You'll feel better for havin' done it." The warden says, sour, "I'll see you in the mornin'!" But Fellenden says, "Oh, no. I'll be gone. I'd explain if I could but you wouldn't believe it. Anyhow, you've been warned, an' you'll take all the precautions anybody could, so nobody can blame you. I like that," says Fellenden. It was funny to hear him talk so quiet an' confident!'

Rodney listened tensely. This was insane, but his body still felt sick and weak with purely physical revulsion against extinction.

'Go on!' said Rodney challengingly.

'The warden says, ironic, "You takin' Limpy?" an' Fellenden says, "I would if I could, Warden. I'd help everybody escape if I could – an' so would you, if you could help 'em escape my way. But everybody has to do it for himself." The warden grunted. He didn't feel easy. Fellenden didn't sound crazy. He wasn't.

Silence, while echoes lingered. Rodney licked his lips.

'In the middle of the night,' Limpy went on, 'the guard come an' looked in Fellenden's cell. I was awake. I hadda reason. I heard Fellenden say, "Good-bye, Clancy. I won't be here when you come back." Clancy says, "I think you will." Him an' Fellenden laughed together. Me, I sweated. I knew what Fellenden was gonna try. After Clancy went out, he says, "I'm startin' Limpy. You try an' make it too. Don't talk to me now." Then it got still. It was so still that I could hear Fellenden breathin'.

He breathed quiet an' steady, quiet an' steady— An' then I didn't hear him breathin' any more. Guy, sweat come out on me in gallons! Next time the guard come through he looked in Fellenden's cell. He jumped a foot. He threw his light in there. Then he yelled. Fellenden was gone. Gone complete. They never found hide nor hair of him. They never even found out how he done it. He was just plain gone!'

There were little dust motes dancing in the shaft of sunlight that came down from overhead. It had moved perceptibly. Rodney said:

'How'd he get out?'

'He didn't,' said Limpy's voice. 'Not out. He got back.'

'To where?' jeered Rodney.

'You shouldda asked when,' said Limpy. He sounded discouraged. 'I shouldn't ha' told you, guy, until you cracked an' were ready to believe. But he went back to the time when he killed his wife. An' then he didn't kill her. He'd found out he was wrong, anyways. So he didn't kill her – an' so he wasn't in the deathhouse for it.'

Rodney swallowed. His eyes fell on the note his lawyers had sent him. They'd done everything that the law or their ingenuity could suggest, and they couldn't do any more. There wasn't any more to do. The sight of that message sent gibbering panic to work at his temples again. But Limpy would hear him. He clenched his hands.

'Why didn't you pull the same trick?' he asked sardonically.

'I tried,' said Limpy. His voice was flat. 'I tried hard. I'm still tryin'. Sometimes I think I'm gonna get it, an' sometimes it seems just crazy. But Fellenden done it. If you could do it, maybe—'

Rodney stood by the bars of his cell. The patch of sunlight was almost near enough for him to reach out his hands and touch it. Presently he would put his hands in it, and feel the warmth of sunshine on his skin. But his hands were shaking.

'It's branching time tracks,' said Rodney, scornfully. 'That's the idea! There can be more than one past, and more than one present, and more than one future. An old speculation. You do something and it sets you on one time track rather than another. If you could go back, you could do something else and get on another time track. That's what Fellenden was talking about.'

'Yeah,' said Limpy tiredly. His voice rolled like the voice of a preacher Rodney had heard once as a child. But his voice was weary. 'Sure! He told me that. You get on a train, he says. It's travelin' through time. Past a town named Monday, an' then past one named Tuesday, an' Wednesday, an' so on. Every so often you change trains. When you get on the wrong train it's bad. He'd got on the wrong train, Fellenden says, when he killed his wife. He hadda go back an' get on the right one. An' he did. But I ain't been able to. I was hopin' maybe—'

Rodney said with a savage humor:

'There's no reason why not! The theory's there. In a multi-dimensional universe, anything imaginable not only could happen, but necessarily must! So Fellenden could, in theory, do what you say he did. The trouble would be that he was on the wrong train. His problem was to get off. How'd he do it? I'm on a train I'd like to get off!'

Suddenly his throat was dry for a new reason. He listened with a desperate intentness for Limpy's answer. The shaft of sunlight was close enough, now, for him to reach, but he did not put out his hands. He licked his lips.

'I said the theory's all right, Limpy! How'd Fellenden do it?'

Limpy said heavily:

'That's where I'm mixed up. You' on a train, he says. It's movin' through time. Before you can go back you got to slow up. But the train won't slow. You see a station slidin' by – Wednesday maybe – an' you wanna go back. You got on the wrong train Tuesday. Desperate, you start runnin' for the back of the train. At first you don't see no difference. But you keep runnin'. Presently the station ain't goin' past you quite so fast. Then you run harder. You hold it even, runnin' with all you got. An' all of a sudden you get to the back of the train. The door's open. You jump down to the tracks, an' don't get hurt because you're runnin' back as fast as the train runs ahead. An' then you go high-tailin' it back along the railroad track to where you got on the wrong train. An' the right one's there—'

'It hasn't left?' asked Rodney, cynically.

'No,' said Limpy flatly. 'I dunno why, but Fellenden said no.'

Rodney's pose of cynicism dropped away. Limpy could not possibly have worked out a theory like this. Fellenden must have worked it out, and phrased it carefully in such homely terms for Limpy's untutored understanding. It was pure logic on a familiar foundation of speculation. You did something, and it had evil consequences. You went back in time, before the event which had the evil consequences. You avoided that event. Then, necessarily, you took a branching time track. You went into another of the innumerable futures which at that point in time were possible for you. The evil consequences of the event you avoided could not be in those other time tracks. And you would cease to exist in the first time track at the point where you turned about and went back.

Granted the fact of time travel in this way, which was the only possible way in which time travel could take place, it was sound! Limpy could not have imagined it. Someone of the caliber of Fellenden must have devised it. And Fellenden had made that indeterminacy field, which nobody else yet surely understood—

Rodney licked his lips. It was the answer, if he could get it – and he had one of the four best brains in the country. But it was enraging that he'd had to be instructed by a common criminal like Limpy!

'I've got it,' said Rodney curtly. 'I see the idea.'

There was a clanking of the outer doors of the death-cell house. A guard came in. He gave the two prisoners their food. Rodney regarded him with the burning eyes of hatred, in silence. The guard went out.

Rodney heard the sounds of Limpy, feeding. Himself, he could not eat. He had three days to live – if he did not solve the problem of time travel as Fellenden had solved it. He could believe in the theory, now. If he did not believe, he would go mad! But besides that, there was evidence that it could be done! Fellenden had done it!

He paced up and down his cell. Time travel. Fellenden had vanished from a death cell in Joliet by traveling back to the time before the killing of his wife. Then he had not killed her. There had been at least two possible futures for him at that point; in one of which he killed her, and in one of which he did not. Rodney lived and moved in the future in which the murder had taken place. In the other – which to Fellenden was now the actual future – Fellenden had not committed a murder, and was doubtless a respected citizen and a prominent physicist instead of an escaped murderer. That other time track was like but not the same as this. It was possible to get into that other time track. Fellenden had done it! Galileo heard that a telescope had been invented, and took thought on the principles of optics, and made a telescope in some ways superior to the original. He, Rodney, now knew that time travel was possible, and he had one of the four best brains—

Time passed. Sweat came out on his forehead. Escape to a parallel time track would be escape of unparalleled completeness. One would have nothing to fear. The very cause of one's fear would no longer be real. Not only the penalty, but the event which called for penalty could be wiped out. But there must be a starting point.

He forgot to put his hands into the slender shaft of sunlight. The sunlight died, and he did not notice it. He paced his cell. Three paces this way. Three paces that. A starting point— A starting point—

It grew dark. Rodney was tense and growing desperate. It was possible! The theory of parallel time tracks was almost orthodox! And Fellenden had proved its verity! But how? Given the beginning, Rodney knew he could go on. Given the principle by which experiment could be made, he could envision every detail that experiment should uncover. But he could not devise a beginning for experiment! He was like someone dying of cold with a fire ready laid but lacking a match, and not knowing how to make a fire drill to produce a spark. It grew maddening!

Night had long fallen when he said sharply into the blackness:

'Limpy!'

He heard Limpy stir.

'Yeah?'

'I've got it,' said Rodney, harshly. 'But I'm curious about Fellenden. Tell me how he started to work. I want to see if I've got a better way than he had?'

Limpy's voice rolled sonorously among the unseen walls.

'You' lyin', guy. A fella who got that trick would want to tell everybody who'd listen.'

Rodney could not imagine it. He snarled:

'Altruism, eh? A part of it is to be kind and good?'

'No!' Limpy spat. Rodney heard him. 'Just – you can't take baggage. Fellenden said so. He said: We got all kinda anchors to this time track we're in – we're hitched tight to the train we're on. We got to cut those bonds loose first. We can't hang on to anything in this time track. It's gonna be imaginary presently. We gotta not care about it any more'n something that's imaginary now. Like' – Limpy's voice was unresentful – 'like you gotta get rid of feelin' proud you got more brains than me. That ties you to me. I'm in this time track. You wanna leave it. You gotta let go of me. I ain't on the train you wanna get!'

In the darkness, Rodney seethed even as this fitted into the pattern of logic. There was a patch of moonlight on the wall above the opposite cell tier. It was the only light anywhere. Limpy's voice rolled on drearily:

'I guess it's no go, guy. I gave you just about all the stuff Fellenden told me. If you can't make it work—' Then Limpy said dubiously, 'There's just one other thing he kinda harped on. He says, how do we know we're on this time track anyhow? How'd we know if we got on another one? What's the difference between 'em, to us? How do we know time's passin'? How do we know we're travelin' in time, anyhow? Does that make sense?'

Rodney's throat hurt when he swallowed.

'B-bishop Berkeley!' he said hoarsely. 'I see and hear and feel the place I'm in. Therefore it is real to me. What I experience is real, to me. What I do not experience—'

Then he cried out. He found himself clutching the bars of his cell. His voice babbled in triumph:

'That's it! That's how you slow yourself in time! Listen! When you listen to a clock tick, seconds are long! When you notice things between the tickings, they're longer! If you speed up your perceptions by noting ever more trivial things, you slow your rate of travel in time! That's the first step!'

His own voice echoed and re-echoed in the darkness. The little patch of moonlight was very sharp and very clear. It was inches from the top of the cell door opposite him. He said exultantly:

'Then you break away from current time entirely. Reality is real because it matters. You've got to push away the mattering of everything in the present. A thing which has no sensible effect has no sensible existence. When you shear away every anchor to the present, you're leaving all baggage behind. In effect, you run to the back of the train, empty-handed and unhindered. When you slow down time and cut every tie with the present, you get ready to jump, to leave— And then you'll be able to change your memory of an event a half-second ago to a perception of an event a half-second ago. And when you've done that, you've won! You've started to travel back in time!'

He shook the bars of his cell, crying exultantly into the darkness. This was logic! This was reason! This was infallibly the experimental method he'd needed! His eyes gleamed.

Limpy's voice came quietly:

'An' then what, guy?'

'Then,' cried Rodney, in exultation, 'when you're no longer anchored to the present by clinging to it, you go back to the last thing you do cling to! You'll have to pick it out before you start! You won't have a chance on the way! You'll think of the moment before you – took the wrong train! You'll stop there! You'll have a chance to take the right train, if you're quick! And then . . . then you'll come back to present parallel time, to this day and hour, but in an alternate existence resulting from the different course you took! Another time track, Limpy! And that's where I'm going to go!'

A long silence. Then Limpy's voice, rumbling soberly in the blackness.

'Yeah . . . I see. Cut loose from now. From everything since the time you wish you'd done different— Yeah! That's it! I didn't realize. I got some cash cached away— All the time I' been tryin' this, I been rememberin' that cache as a stake for me to get started on again. But if I go back to where I gotta go, that stuff won't be on the track my train'll be travelin' on. I got it now—'

Rodney's hands closed tightly on the bars of his cell. He stared at the slowly creeping patch of moonlight. With a fierce satisfaction he listened to his own breathing, noting differences in every breath. He listened, in the monstrous stillness of the deathhouse, to the beating of his own heart.

Limpy's voice came; very grave and very sober.

'I' got to go a long way back. To when I was a kid, I guess. Yeah . . . a long way. All the way!'

Silence. Rodney summoned all the resources of his brain. There were not many brains as good or as disciplined. He knew, and reveled in the knowledge, that all the events that had happened as the consequence of a certain specific instant would soon be unreal. They would be in another time track. They would be might-have-beens, to which no bond could fasten him. Knowing of their coming unreality, he could renounce them. They no longer mattered. They were merely imaginings which would presently have no meaning, and therefore had no meaning now. He viewed them with increasing remoteness, listening to his own breathing and his own heartbeat; watching the creeping patch of moonlight on the wall.

Time slowed. There were intervals between his heartbeats. There were pauses between his breaths. He could distinguish different parts of the heartbeat cycle. He could distinguish parts of the parts— The patch of moonlight ceased to move.

It did not move! There were monstrous intervals between his heartbeats. Triumph filled him. The last instant that counted in his scheme of things was enormously vivid. Nothing was important but that. He clung to the thought of it with a fierce intensity, picturing vividly every detail of it.

The moonlight patch receded a little. It moved with a vast

deliberation – backward! Its rate of movement – backward – increased with a smooth acceleration.

Suddenly there was confusion which was not confusion, and chaos was not chaos at all. It was night and it was day and it was day again. He moved here and there without volition and without effort, like a weightless object upon an insanely charted course at dizzying speed. He was like a phantom on the screen, movable at incredible rates without resistance. Days and nights went by. He flashed through elaborate evolutions with effortless, infinite speed – backward. His speed increased. He could perceive only in flashes. An instant in a car in the open. The car backed with incredible speed. An instant in the courtroom. He was on trial. Flashes of infinitesimal duration before that and before that and before that—

The confusion and the chaos ended suddenly. He was in the room where Professor Adner Hale lay dead. He, Rodney, had committed the murder in the one fashion no one would possibly associate with him. He had done it with insensate, maniacal violence. It seemed the deed of a brutish and almost mindless fiend. It was inconceivable that one of the best brains in the country should have directed senseless, flailing blows which had continued long after Professor Adner Hale was dead. It was a perfect alibi.

And this was the instant when he had made his mistake. He surveyed the blood-spattered, violence-smashed room. He saw a chair which was not overturned in the simulated struggle. He regarded it with satisfaction.

Before, he had toppled it over, without noticing that under it lay the poker with which Professor Hale had been beaten to death. That had been his mistake. It proved that the chair had not been knocked over in Professor Hale's death struggle. It proved that the effect of mania was the result of calculation. It set the police to work to discover, not a maniac but a coldly functioning brain which had duplicated in every detail but that one the working of a homicidal maniac's frenzy. That one small flaw had led to the discovery of clue after clue and the condemnation of the country's greatest physicist to death. But—

Now he laid the chair gently on its side. The poker was *not* under it, now. He pulled gently at a chair leg to bring the poker more plainly into view. Now there was nothing but the handiwork of madness.

He laughed softly. One of the four best brains in the country. He'd been overconfident. That was all. Now this small blunder was corrected. He would go into another time track. The discovery Professor Adner Hale had helped with – on the drudgery only, of course – and which he insisted must be published for all the world to know, would not be published now. With it as his secret, in the time track into which he would now move.

He felt his return to attained time begin. Time moved swiftly. It was dawn, and he was somewhere else. It was night, and he was in another place. Dawn and midday and night. His body whirled here and there and everywhere, without resistance. There was confusion which was not confusion and chaos which was not chaotic at all. While his body whirled frenziedly through the sequence of events which lay between the significant moment and the instant from which he had traveled back – but now he moved in another time track entirely – his mind was calmly exultant. He was in the midst of crowds, and in solitude. He was in a room which flickered like a kaleidoscope – which was a courtroom. There was an instant when he was in a car being driven somewhere. He passed through months in flashes of infinitely short duration. Then--

Time steadied. All was normal again. He was in a cell. In a death cell. It was not the cell he had occupied before, but the death-house was the same. It was dawn, and a gray light came in the skylight high overhead. He wore prison garb – but not the same garments he had worn before. The stenciled numbers were different. He was in a different time track, but he was in a death cell.

There were clankings. Footsteps. Three guards and a trusty appeared before his cell. The trusty, twitching, carried a basin of water and safety razor and a pair of shears. He was to shave Rodney's temples and slit his trouser legs for the convenience of those who would presently – today – take him through that green door and strap him in that horrible squat chair, in which after a little his body – already dead – would struggle convulsively against its doom . . .

He was paralyzed. He could not move. The door of his cell opened. They came in. He could not stir. He barely breathed. He was almost in a coma of pure, incredulous horror.

One of the guards handed him a note.

'Professor Fellenden,' he said curtly, 'you know, the fella who fought so hard for you, got permission to send you this.'

Rodney breathed hoarsely. It was almost impossible to move. For an instant he seemed unconscious of the offered message. Then one of the guards stirred, and he snatched it. They would wait while he read it— They would wait that long. No longer—

His eyes were hard to focus. Almost he did not try to read but only to delay, to gain precious seconds of life. But then he saw an equation, and he reacted with a stunned swiftness. And Fellenden had written down for him, in concise equations and precise, scientific phrasing, the theory of time travel with such absolute clarity that a trained brain could grasp it in a single reading. On the very brink of execution, a scientific mind could comprehend and use this, and escape death by the simple process of going back in time and – not committing murder. But nothing else would suffice. He must not commit murder!

Rodney shifted his eyes and stared unseeingly at the opposite wall. So that was it! He'd been wrong, not in a trivial detail of a murder, but in a basic fact. Execution was a consequence of murder, not of a fumbled clue. And Fellenden, who'd been a murderer himself, had to tell him so with pious urgency! Rodney raged coldly. Very well, he'd go back again! Not to a moment just after he'd murdered Hale, but to a time long before! Before Hale had found out anything for which he would need to be murdered.

The guards lifted him to his feet and bound his hands behind him. He was very calm, now. Ragingly calm. With the clarity of conception that Fellenden had made possible, he knew that it would be infinitely easy to escape. Even in the chair itself. With his brains—

He said scornfully:

'Just for curiosity, I'd like to know what set the police on my trail after the murder. Something trivial – but I've forgotten.'

A guard said awkwardly:

'You laid down a chair to look like it'd been knocked over. You pulled it where you wanted it by one leg. The cops knew it wasn't knocked over because a loose cushion didn't fall out. An' – your fingerprints were on the leg you pulled it by.'

Rodney shrugged. Proof enough. He'd have to go back beyond the murder and not commit it. Too bad! Professor Adner Hale had been a righteous old fool whom it had been a positive pleasure to bludgeon to death. Now he'd have to live in a third time track–

The guards led him out of his cell. He said harshly:

'I'd like to tell Limpy something.' When they stared at him, he said impatiently: 'Limpy Gossett! In the deathhouse, here! I was given a reprieve so it'd be a double execution.'

One of the guards said:

'You didn't get a reprieve, fella. An' there ain't any Limpy Gossett here. Never was. I never heard of 'im.'

The green door opened. Rodney was badly shaken, now. Still, he had only to go back in time. But he gave a precious half-second to a raging hatred of Fellenden, who had written piety in with science in his instructions for Rodney's escape. 'The important thing,' said Fellenden fatuously, 'was to be rid of all ties to the time track you wanted to leave. Everything in it had not to matter to you–' Rodney despised him.

There was the squat and horrible chair. Rodney began to listen to his own breathing. To his own heartbeat. Step by step, they marched him to the chair. Slow down time! Slow it! Watch everything! Cut the things that anchor you to this time track! With that and Fellenden's equations it's easy – but Fellenden's a pious fool!

Time did not slow. He realized it in a surge of panic as they strapped him in the chair. Then he knew why. Fellenden held him in this time track! Fellenden mattered! The fact that he had escaped to here! The equations and the explanation he'd given Rodney could not dismiss them as meaningless! He hated Fellenden with a terrible, despairing hatred. But he had to stop hating him and put all his mind on slowing time–

He fought to achieve it with all the strength of one of the four best brains in the country. He was trying when they drew back from the chair and waited, white-faced, for the switch to be thrown.

He sobbed, then. But he was still trying when—

THE ETHICAL EQUATIONS

Space enigma. In the May, 1945, issue of Astounding Science Fiction *appeared a novelette by Leinster entitled 'First Contact'. It dealt in an entirely new way with the meeting in space of humankind and aliens with an advanced technological background. The story made a great impact at the time: it has appeared in several anthologies, and the problems connected with its filming led to the development of the Jenkins Systems mentioned in the Introduction to this book. 'The Ethical Equations' appeared in the very next issue of* ASF. *It covers a very similar situation – the first contact in deep space with an alien spaceship – but with a very different outcome.*

It is very, very queer. The Ethical Equations, of course, link conduct with probability, and give mathematical proof that certain patterns of conduct increase the probability of certain kinds of coincidences. But nobody ever expected them to have any really practical effect. Elucidation of the laws of chance did not stop gambling, though it did make life insurance practical. The Ethical Equations weren't expected to be even as useful as that. They were just theories, which seemed unlikely to affect anybody particularly. They were complicated, for one thing. They admitted that the ideal pattern of conduct for one man wasn't the best for another. A politician, for example, has an entirely different code – and properly – than a Space Patrol man. But still, on at least one occasion—

The thing from outer space was fifteen hundred feet long, and upward of a hundred and fifty feet through at its middle section, and well over two hundred in a curious bulge like a fish's head at its bow. There were odd, gill-like flaps just back of that bulge, too, and the whole thing looked extraordinarily like a monster, eyeless fish, floating in empty space out beyond Jupiter. But it had drifted in from somewhere beyond the sun's gravitational field – its speed was too great for it to have a closed orbit – and it swung with a slow, inane, purposeless motion about some axis it had established within itself.

The little spacecruiser edged closer and closer. Freddy Holmes had been a pariah on the *Arnina* all the way out from Mars, but he clenched his hands and forgot his misery and the ruin of his career in the excitement of looking at the thing.

'No response to signals on any frequency, sir,' said the communications officer, formally. 'It is not radiating. It has a minute magnetic field. Its surface temperature is just about four degrees absolute.'

The commander of the *Arnina* said, 'Hrrrmph!' Then he said, 'We'll lay alongside.' Then he looked at Freddy Holmes and stiffened. 'No,' he said, 'I believe you take over now, Mr. Holmes.'

Freddy started. He was in a very bad spot, but his excitement had made him oblivious of it for a moment. The undisguised hostility with which he was regarded by the skipper and the others on the bridge brought it back, however.

'You take over, Mr. Holmes,' repeated the skipper bitterly. 'I have orders to that effect. You originally detected this object and your uncle asked Headquarters that you be given full authority to investigate it. You have that authority. Now, what are you going to do with it?'

There was fury in his voice surpassing even the rasping dislike of the voyage out. He was a lieutenant commander and he had been instructed to take orders from a junior officer. That was bad enough. But this was humanity's first contact with an extrasolar civilization, and Freddy Holmes, lieutenant junior grade, had been given charge of the matter by pure political pull.

Freddy swallowed.

'I . . . I—' He swallowed again and said miserably, 'Sir, I've tried to explain that I dislike the present set-up as much as you possibly can. I . . . wish that you would let me put myself under your orders, sir, instead of—'

'No!' rasped the commander vengefully. 'You are in command, Mr. Holmes. Your uncle put on political pressure to arrange it. My orders are to carry out your instructions, not to wet-nurse you if the job is too big for you to handle. This is in your lap! Will you issue orders?'

Freddy stiffened.

'Very well, sir. It's plainly a ship and apparently a derelict. No crew would come in without using a drive, or allow their ship to swing about aimlessly. You will maintain your present position with relation to it. I'll take a spaceboat and a volunteer, if you will find me one, and look it over.'

He turned and left the bridge. Two minutes later he was struggling into a spacesuit when Lieutenant Bridges – also junior grade – came briskly into the spacesuit locker and observed:

'I've permission to go with you, Mr. Holmes.' He began to get into another spacesuit. As he pulled it up over his chest he added blithely: 'I'd say this was worth the price of admission!'

Freddy did not answer. Three minutes later the little spaceboat pulled out from the side of the cruiser. Designed for expeditionary work and tool-carrying rather than as an escapecraft, it was not inclosed. It would carry men in spacesuits, with their tools and weapons, and they could breathe from its tanks instead of from their suits, and use its power and so conserve their own. But it was a strange feeling to sit within its spidery outline and see the great blank sides of the strange object draw near. When the spaceboat actually touched the vast metal wall it seemed impossible, like the approach to some sorcerer's castle across a monstrous moat of stars.

It was real enough, though. The felted rollers touched, and Bridges grunted in satisfaction.

'Magnetic. We can anchor to it. Now what?'

'We hunt for an entrance port,' said Freddy curtly. He added: 'Those openings that look like gills are the drive tubes.

Their drive's in front instead of the rear. Apparently they don't use gyros for steering.'

The tiny craft clung to the giant's skin, like a fly on a stranded whale. It moved slowly to the top of the rounded body, and over it, and down on the other side. Presently the cruiser came in sight again as it came up the near side once more.

'Nary a port, sir,' said Bridges blithely. 'Do we cut our way in?'

'Hm-m-m,' said Freddy slowly. 'We have our drive in the rear, and our control room in front. So we take on supplies amidships, and that's where we looked. But this ship is driven from the front. Its control room might be amidships. If so, it might load at the stern. Let's see.'

The little craft crawled to the stern of the monster.

'There!' said Freddy.

It was not like an entrance port on any vessel in the solar system. It slid aside, without hinges. There was an inner door, but it opened just as readily. There was no rush of air, and it was hard to tell if it was intended as an air lock or not.

'Air's gone,' said Freddy. 'It's a derelict, all right. You might bring a blaster, but what we'll mostly need is light, I think.'

The magnetic anchors took hold. The metal grip shoes of the spacesuits made loud noises inside the suits as the two of them pushed their way into the interior of the ship. The spacecruiser had been able to watch them, until now. Now they were gone.

The giant, enigmatic object which was so much like a blind fish in empty space floated on. It swung aimlessly about some inner axis. The thin sunlight out here beyond Jupiter, smote upon it harshly. It seemed to hang motionless in mid-space against an all-surrounding background of distant and unwinking stars. The trim Space Patrol ship hung alertly a mile and a half away. Nothing seemed to happen at all.

Freddy was rather pale when he went back to the bridge. The pressure mark on his forehead from the spacesuit helmet was still visible, and he rubbed at it abstractedly. The skipper regarded him with a sort of envious bitterness. After all, any human would envy any other who had set foot in an alien spaceship. Lieutenant Bridges followed him. For an instant there were no words. Then Bridges saluted briskly:

'Reporting back on board, sir, and returning to watch duty after permitted volunteer activity.'

The skipper touched his hat sourly. Bridges departed with crisp precision. The skipper regarded Freddy with the helpless fury of a senior officer who has been ordered to prove a junior officer a fool, and who has seen the assignment blow up in his face and that of the superior officers who ordered it. It was an enraging situation. Freddy Holmes, newly commissioned and assigned to the detector station on Luna which keeps track of asteroids and meteor streams, had discovered a small object coming in over Neptune. Its speed was too high for it to be a regular member of the solar system, so he'd reported it as a visitor and suggested immediate examination. But junior officers are not supposed to make discoveries. It violates tradition, which is a sort of Ethical Equation in the Space Patrol. So Freddy was slapped down for his presumption. And he slapped back, on account of the Ethical Equations' bearing upon scientific discoveries. The first known object to come from beyond the stars ought to be examined. Definitely. So, most unprofessionally for a Space Patrol junior, Freddy raised a stink.

The present state of affairs was the result. He had an uncle who was a prominent politican. That uncle went before the Space Patrol Board and pointed out smoothly that his nephew's discovery was important. He demonstrated with mathematical precision that the Patrol was being ridiculous in ignoring a significant discovery simply because a junior officer had made it. And the Board, seething at outside interference, ordered Freddy to be taken to the object he had detected, given absolute command of the spacecruiser which had taken him there, and directed to make the examination he had suggested. By all the laws of probability, he would have to report that the hunk of matter from beyond the solar system was just like hunks of matter in it. And then the Board would pin back both his and his uncle's ears with a vengeance.

But now the hunk of matter turned out to be a fish-shaped artifact from an alien civilization. It turned out to be important. So the situation was one to make anybody steeped in Patrol tradition grind his teeth.

'The thing, sir,' said Freddy evenly, 'is a spaceship. It is driven by atomic engines shooting blasts sternward from somewhere near the bow. Apparently they steer only by hand. Apparently, too, there was a blow-up in the engine room and they lost most of their fuel out the tube vents. After that, the ship was helpless though they patched up the engines after a fashion. It is possible to calculate that in its practically free fall to the sun it's been in its present state for a couple of thousand years.'

'I take it, then,' said the skipper with fine irony, 'that there are no survivors of the crew.'

'It presents several problems, sir,' said Freddy evenly, 'and that's one of them.' He was rather pale. 'The ship is empty of air, but her tanks are full. Storage spaces containing what look like supplies are only partly emptied. The crew did not starve or suffocate. The ship simply lost most of her fuel. So it looks like they prepared the ship to endure an indefinite amount of floating about in free space and' – he hesitated – 'then it looks like they went into suspended animation. They're all on board, in transparent cases that have – machinery attached. Maybe they thought they'd be picked up by sister ships sooner or later.'

The skipper blinked.

'Suspended animation? They're alive?' Then he said sharply: 'What sort of ship is it? Cargo?'

'No, sir.' said Freddy. 'That's another problem. Bridges and I agree that it's a fighting ship, sir. There are rows of generators serving things that could only be weapons. By the way they're braced, there are tractor beams and pressor beams and – there are vacuum tubes that have grids but apparently work with cold cathodes. By the size of the cables that lead to them, those tubes handle amperages up in the thousands. You can figure that one out, sir.'

The skipper paced two steps this way, and two steps that. The thing was stupendous. But his instructions were precise.

'I'm under your orders,' he said doggedly. 'What are you going to do?'

'I'm going to work myself to death, I suppose,' said Freddy unhappily, 'and some other men with me. I want to go over that ship backwards, forwards, and sideways with scanners, and everything the scanners see photographed back on board, here. I want men to work the scanners and technicians on board to direct them for their specialties. I want to get every rivet and coil in that whole ship on film before touching anything.'

The skipper said grudgingly:

'That's not too foolish. Very well, Mr. Holmes, it will be done.'

'Thank you,' said Freddy. He started to leave the bridge, and stopped. 'The men to handle the scanners,' he added, 'ought to be rather carefully picked. Imaginative men wouldn't do. The crew of that ship – they look horribly alive, and they aren't pretty. And . . . er . . . the plastic cases they're in are arranged to open from inside. That's another problem still, sir.'

He went on down. The skipper clasped his hands behind his back and began to pace the bridge furiously. The first object from beyond the stars was a spaceship. It had weapons the Patrol had only vainly imagined. And he, a two-and-a-half striper, had to stand by and take orders for its investigation from a lieutenant junior grade just out of the Academy. Because of politics! The skipper ground his teeth—

Then Freddy's last comment suddenly had meaning. The plastic cases in which the alien's crew lay in suspended animation opened from the inside. From the inside!

Cold sweat came out on the skipper's forehead as he realized the implication. Tractor and pressor beams, and the ship's fuel not quite gone, and the suspended-animation cases opening from the inside—

There was a slender, coaxial cable connecting the two spacecraft, now. They drifted in sunward together. The little cruiser was dwarfed by the alien giant.

The sun was very far away; brighter than any star, to be sure, and pouring out a fierce radiation, but still very far from a warming orb. All about were the small, illimitably distant lights which were stars. There was exactly one object in view which had an appreciable diameter. That was Jupiter, a new moon in shape, twenty million miles sunward and eighty million miles farther along its orbit. The rest was emptiness.

The spidery little spaceboat slid along the cable between the two craft. Spacesuited figures got out and clumped on magnetic-soled shoes to the air lock. They went in.

Freddy came to the bridge. The skipper said hoarsely:

'Mr. Holmes, I would like to make a request. You are, by orders of the Board, in command of this ship until your investigation of the ship yonder is completed.'

Freddy's face was haggard and worn. He said abstractedly:

'Yes, sir. What is it?'

'I would like,' said the *Arnina*'s skipper urgently, 'to send a complete report of your investigation so far. Since you are in command, I cannot do so without your permission.'

'I would rather you didn't, sir,' said Freddy. Tired as he was his jaws clamped. 'Frankly, sir, I think they'd cancel your present orders and issue others entirely.'

The skipper bit his lip. That was the idea. The scanners had sent back complete images of almost everything in the other ship, now. Everything was recorded on film. The skipper had seen the monsters which were the crew of the extrasolar vessel. And the plastic cases in which they had slumbered for at least two thousand years did open from the inside. That was what bothered him. They did open from the inside!

The electronics technicians of the *Arnina* were going about in stilly rapture, drawing diagrams for each other and contemplating the results with dazed appreciation. The gunnery officer was making scale, detailed design-drawings for weapons he had never hoped for, and waking up of nights to feel for those drawings and be sure that they were real. But the engineer officer was wringing his hands. He wanted to take the other ship's engines apart. They were so enormously smaller than the *Arnina*'s drive, and yet they had driven a ship with eighty-four times the *Arnina*'s mass – and he could not see how they could work.

The alien ship was ten thousand years ahead of the *Arnina*. Its secrets were being funneled over to the little Earth-ship at a rapid rate. But the cases holding its still-living crew opened from the inside.

'Nevertheless, Mr. Holmes,' the skipper said feverishly, 'I must ask permission to send that report.'

'But I am in command,' said Freddy tiredly, 'and I intend to stay in command. I will give you a written order forbidding you to make a report, sir. Disobedience will be mutiny.'

The skipper grew almost purple.

'Do you realize,' he demanded savagely, 'that if the crew of that ship is in suspended animation, and if their coffins or containers open only from inside – do you realize that they expect to open them themselves?'

'Yes, sir,' said Freddy wearily. 'Of course. Why not?'

'Do you realize that cables from those containers lead to thermobatteries in the ship's outer plating? The monsters knew they couldn't survive without power, but they knew that in any other solar system they could get it! So they made sure they'd pass close to our sun with what power they dared use, and went into suspended animation with a reserve of power to land on and thermobatteries that would waken them when it was time to set to work!'

'Yes, sir,' said Freddy, as wearily as before. 'They had courage, at any rate. But what would you do about that?'

'I'd report it to Headquarters!' raged the skipper. 'I'd report that this is a warship capable of blasting the whole Patrol out of the ether and smashing our planets! I'd say it was manned by monsters now fortunately helpless, but with fuel enough to maneuver to a landing. And I'd ask authority to take their coffins out of their ship and destroy them! Then I'd—'

'I did something simpler,' said Freddy. 'I disconnected the thermobatteries. They can't revive. So I'm going to get a few hours' sleep. If you'll excuse me—'

He went to his own cabin and threw himself on his bunk.

Men with scanners continued to examine every square inch of the monster derelict. They worked in spacesuits. To have filled the giant hull with air would practically have emptied the *Arnina*'s tanks. A spacesuited man held a scanner before a curious roll of flexible substance, on which were inscribed symbols. His headphones brought instructions from the photo room. A record of some sort was being duplicated by photography. There were scanners at work in the storerooms, the crew's quarters, the gun mounts. So far no single article had been moved from the giant stranger. That was Freddy's order. Every possible bit of information was being extracted from every possible object, but nothing had been taken away. Even chemical analysis was being done by scanner, using cold-light spectrography applied from the laboratory on the cruiser.

And Freddy's unpopularity had not lessened. The engineer officer cursed him luridly. The stranger's engines, now— They had been patched up after an explosion, and they were tantalizingly suggestive. But their working was unfathomable. The engineer officer wanted to get his hands on them. The physio-chemical officer wanted to do some analysis with his own hands, instead of by cold-light spectrography over a scanner. And every man, from the lowest enlisted apprentice to the skipper himself, wanted to get hold of some artifact made by an alien, non-human race ten thousand years ahead of human civilization. So Freddy was unpopular.

But that was only part of his unhappiness. He felt that he had acted improperly. The Ethical Equations gave mathematical proof that probabilities and ethics are interlinked, so that final admirable results cannot be expected from unethical beginnings. Freddy had violated discipline – which is one sort of ethics – and after that through his uncle had interjected politics into Patrol affairs. Which was definitely a crime. By the Equations, the probability of disastrous coincidences was going to be enormous until corrective, ethically proper action was taken to cancel out the original crimes. And Freddy had been unable to devise such action. He felt, too, that the matter was urgent. He slept uneasily despite his fatigue, because there was something in the back of his mind which warned him stridently that disaster lay ahead.

Freddy awoke still unrefreshed and stared dully at the

ceiling over his head. He was trying discouragedly to envision a reasonable solution when there came a tap on his door. It was Bridges with a batch of papers.

'Here you are!' he said cheerfully, when Freddy opened to him. 'Now we're all going to be happy!'

Freddy took the extended sheets.

'What's happened?' he asked. 'Did the skipper send for fresh orders regardless, and I'm to go in the brig?'

Bridges, grinning, pointed to the sheets of paper in Freddy's hand. They were from the physiochemical officer, who was equipped to do exact surveys on the lesser heavenly bodies.

'*Elements found in the alien vessel,*' was the heading of a list. Freddy scanned the list. No heavy elements, but the rest was familiar. There had been pure nitrogen in the fuel tank, he remembered, and the engineer officer was going quietly mad trying to understand how they had used nitrogen for atomic power. Freddy looked down to the bottom. Iron was the heaviest element present.

'Why should this make everybody happy?' asked Freddy.

Bridges pointed with his finger. The familiar atomic symbols had unfamiliar numerals by them. H^3, Li^5, Gl^8— He blinked He saw N^{15}, F^{18}, $S^{34,35}$— Then he stared. Bridges grinned.

'Try to figure what that ship's worth!' he said happily. 'It's all over the *Arnina*. Prize money isn't allowed in the Patrol, but five percent of salvage is. Hydrogen three has been detected on Earth, but never isolated. Lithium five doesn't exist on Earth, or glucinium eight, or nitrogen fifteen or oxygen seventeen or fluorine eighteen or sulphur thirty-four or thirty-five! The whole ship is made up of isotopes that simply don't exist in the solar system! And you know what pure isotopes sell for! The hull's practically pure iron fifty-five! Pure iron fifty-four sells for thirty-five credits a gram! Talk about the lost treasures of Mars! For technical use only, the stripped hull of this stranger is worth ten years' revenue of Earth government! Every man on the *Arnina* is rich for life. And you're popular!'

Freddy did not smile.

'Nitrogen fifteen,' he said slowly. 'That's what's in the remaining fuel tank. It goes into a queer little aluminum chamber we couldn't figure out, and from there into the drive tubes. I see—'

He was very pale. Bridges beamed.

'A hundred thousand tons of materials that simply don't exist on Earth! Pure isotopes, intact! Not a contamination in a carload! My dear chap, I've come to like you, but you've been hated by everyone else. Now come out and bask in admiration and affection!'

Freddy said, unheeding:

'I've been wondering what that aluminium chamber was for. It looked so infernally simple, and I couldn't see what it did—'

'Come out and have a drink!' insisted Bridges joyously. 'Be lionized! Make friends and influence people!'

'No,' said Freddy. He smiled mirthlessly. 'I'll be lynched later anyhow. Hm-m-m. I want to talk to the engineer officer. We want to get that ship navigating under its own power. It's too big to do anything with towlines.'

'But nobody's figured out its engines!' protested Bridges. 'Apparently there's nothing but a tiny trickle of nitrogen through a silly chamber that does something to it, and then it flows through aluminum baffles into the drive tubes. It's too simple! How are you going to make a thing like that work?'

'I think,' said Freddy, 'it's going to be horribly simple. That whole ship is made up of isotopes we don't have on Earth. No. It has aluminum and carbon. They're simple substances. Theirs and ours are just alike. But most of the rest—'

He was pale. He looked as if he were suffering.

'I'll get a couple of tanks made up, of aluminum, and filled with nitrogen. Plain air should do— And I'll want a gyro-control. I'll want it made of aluminum, too, with graphite bearings—'

He grinned mirthlessly at Bridges.

'Ever hear of the Ethical Equations, Bridges? You'd never expect them to suggest the answer to a space-drive problem, would you? But that's what they've done. I'll get the engineer officer to have those things made up. It's nice to have known you, Bridges—'

As Bridges went out, Freddy Holmes sat down, wetting his lips, to make sketches for the engineer officer to work from.

The control room and the engine room of the monster ship were one. It was a huge, globular chamber filled with apparatus of startlingly alien design. To Freddy, and to Bridges too, now, there was not so much of monstrousness as at first. Eight days of familiarity, and knowledge of how they worked, had made them seem almost normal. But still it was eerie to belt themselves before the instrument board, with only their hand lamps for illumination, and cast a last glance at the aluminum replacements of parts that had been made on some planet of another sun.

'If this works,' said Freddy, and swallowed, 'we're lucky. Here's the engine control. Cross your fingers, Bridges.'

The interior of the hulk was still airless. Freddy shifted a queerly shaped lever an infinitesimal trace. There was a slight surging movement of the whole vast hull. A faint murmuring came through the fabric of the monster ship to the soles of their spacesuit boots. Freddy wet his lips and touched another lever.

'This should be lights.'

It was. Images formed on the queerly shaped screens. The whole interior of the ship glowed. And the whole creation had been so alien as somehow to be revolting, in the harsh white light of the hand lamps the men had used. But now it was like a highly improbable fairy palace. The fact that all doors were circular and all passages round tubes was only pleasantly strange, in the many-colored glow of the ship's own lighting system. Freddy shook his head in his spacesuit helmet, as if to shake away drops of sweat on his forehead.

'The next should be heat,' he said more grimly than before. 'We do not touch that! Oh, definitely! But we try the drive.'

The ship stirred. It swept forward in a swift smooth acceleration that was invincibly convincing of power. The *Arnina* dwindled swiftly, behind. And Freddy, with compressed lips, touched controls here, and there, and the monstrous ship obeyed with the docility of a willing, well-trained animal. It swept back to clear sight of the *Arnina*.

'I would say,' said Bridges in a shaking voice, 'that it works. The Patrol has nothing like this!'

'No,' said Freddy shortly. His voice sounded sick. 'Not like this! It's a sweet ship. I'm going to hook in the gyro controls. They ought to work. The creatures who made this didn't use them. I don't know why. But they didn't.'

He cut off everything but the lights. He bent down and looked in the compact little aluminum device which would control the flow of nitrogen to the port and starboard drive tubes.

Freddy came back to the control board and threw in the drive once more. And the gyro control worked. It should. After all, the tool work of a Space Patrol machinist should be good. Freddy tested it thoroughly. He set it on a certain fine adjustment. He threw three switches. Then he picked up one tiny kit he had prepared.

'Come along,' he said tiredly. 'Our work's over. We go back to the *Arnina* and I probably get lynched.'

Bridges, bewildered, followed him to the spidery little spaceboat. They cast off from the huge ship, now three miles or more from the *Arnina* and untenanted save by its own monstrous crew in suspended animation. The Space Patrol cruiser shifted position to draw near and pick them up. And Freddy said hardly:

'Remember the Ethical Equations, Bridges? I said they gave me the answer to that other ship's drive. If they were right, it couldn't have been anything else. Now I'm going to find out about something else.'

His spacegloved hands worked clumsily. From the tiny kit he spilled out a single small object. He plopped it into something from a chest in the spaceboat – a mortar shell, as Bridges saw incredulously. He dropped that into the muzzle of a line-mortar the spaceboat carried as a matter of course. He jerked the lanyard. The mortar flamed. Expanding gases beat at the spacesuits of the men. A tiny, glowing, crimson spark sped toward outer space. Seconds passed. Three. Four. Five—

'Apparently I'm a fool,' said Freddy, in the grimmest voice Bridges had ever heard.

But then there was light. And such light! Where the dwindling red spark of a tracer mortar shell had sped toward infinitely distant stars, there was suddenly an explosion of such incredible violence as even the proving-grounds of the Space Patrol had never known. There was no sound in empty space. There was no substance to be heated to incandescence other than that of a half-pound tracer shell. But there was a flare of blue-white light and a crash of such violent static that Bridges was deafened by it. Even through the glass of his helmet he felt a flash of savage heat. Then there was – nothing.

'What was that?' said Bridges, shaken.

'The Ethical Equations,' said Freddy. 'Apparently I'm not the fool I thought—'

The *Arnina* slid up alongside the little spaceboat. Freddy did not alight. He moved the boat over to its cradle and plugged in his communicator set. He talked over that set with his helmet phone, not radiating a signal that Bridges could pick up. In three minutes or so the great lock opened and four space-suited figures came out. One wore the crested four-communicator helmet which only the skipper of a cruiser wears when in command of a landing party. The newcomers to the outside of the *Arnina*'s hull crowded into the little spaceboat. Freddy's voice sounded again in the headphones, grim and cold.

'I've some more shells, sir. They're tracer shells which have been in the work boat for eight days. They're not quite as cold as the ship, yonder – that's had two thousand years to cool off in – but they're cold. I figure they're not over eight or ten degrees absolute. And here are the bits of material from the other ship. You can touch them. Our spacesuits are as nearly non-conductive of heat as anything could be. You won't warm them if you hold them in your hand.'

The skipper – Bridges could see him – looked at the scraps of metal Freddy held out to him. They were morsels of iron and other material from the alien ship. By the cold glare of a hand-light the skipper thrust one into the threaded hollow at the nose of a mortar shell into which a line-end is screwed when a line is to be thrown. The skipper himself dropped in the mortar shell and fired it. Again a racing, receding speck of red in emptiness. And a second terrible, atomic blast.

The skipper's voice in the headphones:

'How much more of the stuff did you bring away?'

'Three more pieces, sir,' said Freddy's voice, very steady now. 'You see how it happens, sir. They're isotopes we don't have on Earth. And we don't have them because in contact with other isotopes at normal temperatures, they're unstable. They go off. Here we dropped them into the mortar shells and nothing happened, because both isotopes were cold – down to the temperature of liquid helium, or nearly. But there's a tracer compound in the shells, and it burns as they fly away. The shell grows warm. And when either isotope, in contact with the other, is as warm as ... say ... liquid hydrogen ... why ... they destroy each other. The ship yonder is of the same material. Its mass is about a hundred thousand tons. Except for the aluminum and maybe one or two other elements that also are nonisotopic and the same in both ships, every bit of that ship will blast off if it comes in contact with matter from this solar system above ten or twelve degrees absolute.'

'Shoot the other samples away,' said the skipper harshly. 'We want to be sure—'

There were three violent puffs of gases expanding into empty space. There were three incredible blue-white flames in the void. There was silence. Then—

'That thing has to be destroyed,' said the skipper, heavily. 'We couldn't set it down anywhere, and its crew might wake up anyhow, at any moment. We haven't anything that could fight it, and if it tried to land on Earth—'

The alien monster, drifting aimlessly in the void, suddenly moved. Thin flames came from the gill-like openings at the bow. Then one side jetted more strongly. It swung about, steadied, and swept forward with a terrifying smooth acceleration. It built up speed vastly more swiftly than any Earthship could possibly do. It dwindled to a speck. It vanished in empty space.

But it was not bound inward toward the sun. It was not headed for the plainly visible half-moon disk of Jupiter, now barely seventy million miles away. It headed out toward the stars.

'I wasn't sure until a few minutes ago,' said Freddy Holmes unsteadily, 'but by the Ethical Equations something like that was probable. I couldn't make certain until we'd gotten everything possible from it, and until I had everything arranged. But I was worried from the first. The Ethical Equations made it pretty certain that if we did the wrong thing we'd suffer for it . . . and by we I mean the whole Earth, because any visitor from beyond the stars would be bound to affect the whole human race.' His voice wavered a little. 'It was hard to figure out what we ought to do. If one of our ships had been in the same fix, though, we'd have hoped for – friendliness. We'd hope for fuel, maybe, and help in starting back home. But this ship was a warship, and we'd have been helpless to fight it. It would have been hard to be friendly. Yet, according to the Ethical Equations, if we wanted our first contact with an alien civilization to be of benefit to us, it was up to us to get it started back home with plenty of fuel.'

'You mean,' said the skipper, incredulously, 'you mean you—'

'Its engines use nitrogen,' said Freddy. 'It runs nitrogen fifteen into a little gadget we know how to make, now. It's very simple, but it's a sort of atom smasher. It turns nitrogen fifteen into nitrogen fourteen and hydrogen. I think we can make use of that for ourselves. Nitrogen fourteen is the kind we have. It can be handled in aluminum pipes and tanks, because there's only one aluminum, which is stable under all conditions. But when it hits the alien isotopes in the drive tubes, it breaks down—'

He took a deep breath.

'I gave them a double aluminum tank of nitrogen, and bypassed their atom smasher. Nitrogen fourteen goes into their drive tubes, and they drive! And . . . I figured back their orbit, and set a gyro to head them back for their own solar system for as long as the first tank of nitrogen holds out. They'll make it out of the sun's gravitational field on that, anyhow. And I reconnected their thermobatteries. When they start to wake up they'll see the gyro and know that somebody gave it to them.

The double tank is like their own and they'll realize they have a fresh supply of fuel to land with. It . . . may be a thousand years before they're back home, but when they get there they'll know we're friendly and . . . not afraid of them. And meanwhile we've got all their gadgets to work on and work with—'

Freddy was silent. The little spaceboat clung to the side of the *Arnina,* which with its drive off was now drifting in sunward past the orbit of Jupiter.

'It is very rare,' said the skipper ungraciously, 'that a superior officer in the Patrol apologizes to an inferior. But I apologize to you, Mr. Holmes, for thinking you a fool. And when I think that I, and certainly every other Patrol officer of experience, would have thought of nothing but setting that ship down at Patrol Base for study, and when I think what an atomic explosion of a hundred thousand tons of matter would have done to Earth . . . I apologize a second time.'

Freddy said uncomfortably:

'If there are to be any apologies made, sir, I guess I've got to make them. Every man on the *Arnina* has figured he's rich, and I've sent it all back where it came from. But you see, sir, the Ethical Equations—'

When Freddy's resignation went in with the report of his investigation of the alien vessel, it was returned marked '*Not Accepted*'. And Freddy was ordered to report to a tiny, hard-worked spacecan on which a junior Space Patrol officer normally gets his ears pinned back and learns his work the hard way. And Freddy was happy, because he wanted to be a Space Patrol officer more than he wanted anything else in the world. His uncle was satisfied, too, because he wanted Freddy to be content, and because certain space-admirals truculently told him that Freddy was needed in the Patrol and would get all the consideration and promotion he needed without any politicians butting in. And the Space Patrol was happy because it had a lot of new gadgets to work with which were going to make it a force able not only to look after interplanetary traffic but defend it, if necessary.

And, for that matter, the Ethical Equations were satisfied.

SYMBIOSIS

War. Leinster tackled this theme often, and in a variety of ways. At the time that this story appeared he had just written 'The Murder of the U.S.A.' for Argosy *magazine. The fact that this item first appeared in* Collier's *is a reminder that Leinster wrote well over a thousand stories for* general *publication. It is very much the type of story that he wrote so well, leaving one thinking 'if only it were possible . . .'*

SURGEON GENERAL MORS was out in the rural districts of Kantolia Province, patiently arguing peasants into allowing the vaccination of their pigs and the inoculation of their families, when the lightning occupation took place.

There was no declaration of war, of course. Parachutists simply began to drop out of a predawn sky an hour before sunrise; at the same time, jet planes sprayed the quiet empty streets of Stadheim, the provincial capital, with machine-gun bullets, which killed two dogs and a stray cat. Then roaring, motorized columns raced across the international bridge at Balt. Armed men rounded up the drowsy customs guards and held them prisoner while tanks, armored cars, and all the impressive panoply of war drove furiously into the still peacefully sleeping countryside. Then armored trains chuffed impressively across the international line, their whistles bellowing defiance to the switch engines and handcars in the Kantolian engine yards. A splendid, totally unheralded stroke of conquest began in the cold gray light of early morning.

When dawn actually arrived and the people of Kantolia began to wake in their beds, more than half of the province was already in enemy hands. The few enemy casualties occurred in a railroad wreck, which itself was due to the action of over-enthusiastic quislings who blew up a railroad bridge to prevent the arrival of defending troops. That action merely held up the invasion program by two hours and a half in that sector. By eight o'clock of a drowsy, sunny morning, the province of Kantolia had been taken over.

Surgeon General Mors heard about it at nine, while he stood beside a pigsty and patiently argued with a peasant who had so far refused to allow either his pigs or his family to be inoculated. Mors heard the news in silence. Then he turned heavily to the civilian doctor with him.

'I had not much hope, but it is very bad,' he said. 'War is always bad! And I hoped so much that we would finish our program of immunization! No nation before has ever achieved one hundred per cent inoculation. It would have been a very great achievement.'

Standing beside the pigsty he wiped his forehead. 'Now, of course, I shall have to go to Stadheim. That will be the enemy headquarters, no doubt. I hope, Doctor, that you will continue the inoculation program while you can. I beg you to do so! One hundred per cent immunization in even a single province would be a great feat! And after all, it is not as if the enemy would not be driven out. But even in ten days terrible damage can be done!'

He went to the small, battered car in which he had been making his rounds, arguing with stubborn peasants. He was a stocky little man with deep circles under his eyes – somehow officials of small nations located close to a large one with visions of military glory tend not to sleep well of nights. Surgeon General Mors had not slept well for a long time.

Perhaps, as a military officer, he should have tried to rejoin the defending army which so far had not fired a shot. But his presence in this region had been to further the inoculation program, and that program had locally been directed from Stadheim.

As his car bumped and whined along the highway toward the provincial capital, the occupation progressed all about him without actually touching him. Three times he heard flights of jet planes roaring through the clear blue sky above. He could not pick them out because of their speed. Once he saw a faraway cloud of dust which was an armored column racing for some strategic spot not yet taken over. The enemy acted as if Kantolia had bristled with troops and weapons, instead of being defended only by customs guards at the border and the fifteen-man police force of Stadheim.

The little car clanked and sputtered. The morning was quite perfect. Here and there a cotton wool cloud floated in the blue. All about were green tablelands, spread with lusty growing crops. Surgeon General Mors looked almost enviously at the unconcerned people of the rustic villages through which he passed. They had no desire for war, and most of them did not yet know that it had come. He felt that any conceivable means was permissible for the defense of simple people like these against the alleged ideals of the enemy. But he looked very unhappy indeed.

Toward noon, he saw the steeples of Stadheim before him. But he turned abruptly aside as if to postpone the inevitable. He drove up a gentle, rolling incline until he came to the squat, functional building which housed the pumping station for the provincial city's water supply. The station and its surroundings seemed untouched, but when the engineer of the pumping station came out, the surgeon general could tell by his expression that he knew of the tragedy that had struck the country.

Surgeon General Mors got out of the car.

'They have not come here yet,' he said in a flat, matter-of-fact voice.

'Not yet,' said the engineer. He ground his teeth. 'I have carried out my orders,' he said harshly. 'Just as I was told.'

Surgeon General Mors nodded.

'That is good.' Then he hesitated. 'I would like to look over the plant,' he said almost apologetically. 'It is very modern and clean. The – enemy spent their money on guns. They might try to remove it for one of their cities.'

The engineer stood aside. Surgeon General Mors went through the little pumping plant. There were only twenty thousand people in Stadheim, so a large installation was not required, but it was sound and practical. There were the filters, and the chlorination apparatus, and the well-equipped small laboratory for tests of the water's purity. The people of Stadheim would always have good water to drink, if the invaders didn't wreck or remove this machinery.

'It is good,' said the stocky little man unhappily, 'to see things like this. It makes for people to be healthy, and therefore happy. Do you know,' he added irrelevantly, 'that our inoculation program was almost one hundred per cent complete? Ah, well—' He paused. 'I must go on to Stadheim. The invaders are there. I shall try to reason with them about our sanitary arrangements. Their soldiers will not understand how careful we are about sanitation. I shall try to get them not to make changes while they are here.'

The engineer's eyes burned suddenly.

'While they are here!'

'Yes,' Surgeon General Mors went on disconsolately. 'They will not stay more than ten days. War is very terrible! It is everything that we doctors fight against all our lives. But so long as men do not understand, there must be wars.' He drew a deep, unhappy breath. 'It will indeed be terrible! May it be the last.'

There was a sudden change in the engineer's eyes.

'Then we fight? My orders—'

'Yes,' said Surgeon General Mors, reluctantly. 'In our own way, we fight. In the only way a small nation can defend itself against a great one. We may need as long as ten days before we drive them out, and when it comes it will be a very terrible victory!'

He hesitated, and then spread out his hands in a gesture of helplessness. He walked out to the car and drove sturdily toward Stadheim.

Sentries stopped him at the outskirts of the city, to confiscate the car. But when he got out wearing the uniform of his country's military force, he was immediately arrested. He was marched toward the center of the city by a soldier who held a bayonet pressing lightly against the small of the little man's back. Mors, of course, was of the medical branch of his army and looked hopelessly unmilitary, and he carried no weapon more dangerous than a fountain pen. But the enemy soldier felt like a conqueror, and this was his first chance to act the part.

When the surgeon general of his country's army was taken to the general commanding the invading troops, the latter was already much annoyed. There had not been a single shot fired in the invasion, and this time the history books would place the credit where it belonged – with the dull, anonymous men who had prepared timetables and traffic control orders, rather than with the combat leadership. General Vladek would go down in history, if at all, only as the nominal leader of an intricate cross-country troop movement. This he did not like.

An hour since, too, he had performed an impressive ceremony on a balcony of the provincial capitol building. With officers flanking him and troops drawn up in the square below, he had read a proclamation to the people of Kantolia. They had been redeemed, said the proclamation, from the grinding oppression of their native country; henceforth they would enjoy all the blessings of oppressive taxes and secret police enjoyed by the invaders. They should rejoice, because now they were citizens of their great neighbor – and anybody who did not rejoice was very likely to be shot. In short, General Vladek had read a proclamation annexing Kantolia to his own country, and he felt very much like a fool. It was not exactly a gala occasion. But the only witnesses outside of his own troops had been two gaping street sweepers and a little knot of twenty quislings who tried to make their cheers atone for the silence of the twenty thousand people who stayed away.

However, when Surgeon General Mors was brought to his office as a prisoner of war, General Vladek felt a little better. A general officer taken prisoner! *This* had some of the savor of traditional war! The prisoner, of course, was a stocky, short figure in a badly fitting uniform, and his broad features indicated peasant ancestry. But General Vladek tried to make the most of the situation with military courtesy.

'I offer my apologies,' said General Vladek grandly, 'if you were subjected to any discourtesy at the time of your capture, my dear General. But after all' – he smiled condescendingly – 'this is war!'

'Is it?' asked Mors. He continued in a businesslike tone: 'I was not sure. When was the declaration of war issued, and by whom?'

General Vladek blinked.

'Why – ah – no formal declaration was made by my government. There were military reasons for secrecy.'

Surgeon General Mors sat down and mopped his face.

'Ah! I am relieved. If you invaded without a declaration of war, you have the legal status of a bandit. Naturally, my government would not regularize your position. Even as a bandit, however,' he said prosaically, 'you will understand that the local sanitary arrangements should not be interfered with. That was what I came to see you about. My country has the lowest death rate in all Europe, and any meddling with our health services would be very stupid. I hope you will give orders—'

General Vladek roared. Then he calmed himself, fuming. 'I did not receive you to be lectured,' he said stiffly. 'So far as I am aware, you are the ranking officer of your army to be captured by my men. I make a formal demand for the surrender of all troops under your command.'

'But there aren't any!' said Surgeon General Mors in surprise. 'My government would not be so imbecilic as to leave soldiers in a province they were not strong enough to defend! They'd only have been killed in trumped-up fighting so you could claim a victory!'

General Vladek's eyes glittered. He pounced.

'Ha! Then your government knew that we intended to invade?'

'My dear man!' said Mors with some tartness. 'Your government has been drooling at the mouth for years over the fact that the taxes from our richest province would almost balance its budget! Of course we suspected you would someday try to seize it! We are not altogether fools!'

'Yet,' said General Vladek sardonically, 'you did not prepare to defend it!'

Surgeon General Mors blinked at the slim, bemedaled figure of his official captor.

'When a peaceful householder hears a burglar in his house,' he said shortly, 'he may or may not go to fight himself, but he does not send his young sons! If he is sensible, he sends for the police.'

'He sends for the police!' repeated Vladek incredulously. 'My good Surgeon General Mors, do you expect the United Nations to interfere in this matter? The United Nations is run by diplomats, phrasemakers. They are aghast and helpless before an accomplished fact like our actual possession of Kantolia! My good sir—'

'This talk is nonsense!' said Mors irritably. 'I came to offer you the benefit of my experience in matters of military and public health. Do you have the welfare of your men actually at heart?'

There was a pause. General Vladek was slim and beautifully tailored. He did not belong in the office of the provincial governor of Kantolia, whose desk was still littered with papers concerning such local affairs as the price of pigs and crops and an outbreak of measles in the public schools. The office was slightly grubby, despite a certain plebeian attempt at elegance. General Vladek seemed fastidiously detached from his surroundings. And he was amused.

'I assure you,' said General Vladek, 'that I am duly solicitous of my men's health.'

'If you are solicitous enough,' said Surgeon General Mors curtly, 'you will get them out of here as quickly as they came in! But I can hardly expect you to comply with that wish. What I have to say is that your troops had better have as little to do with the civilian population as possible – no communication of any sort that can possibly be avoided.'

'You are ridiculous,' said General Vladek, annoyed. 'Kantolia is now part of my country. Its people are the fellow citizens of my troops. Isolate them? Ridiculous!'

Surgeon General Mors stood up and shrugged.

'Very well,' he said heavily. 'I advised you. Now, either I am a prisoner or I am not. If not, I would like a pass allowing me to go about freely. The sudden entry of so large an invading force introduces problems of public health—'

'Which my medical corps,' said General Vladek scornfully, 'is quite able to cope with! You are a prisoner, and I think a fool! Good day!'

Surgeon General Mors marched stolidly to the door. . . .

Since the invasion was not yet one day old, there had been no time to build concentration camps. Surgeon General Mors was confined, therefore, in a school which had been closed to education that it might be taken over and used as a prison. He found himself in company with the provincial governor of Kantolia, with the mayor of Stadheim, and various other officials arrested by the invaders. There were private citizens in confinement, too – mostly people whom the small number of quislings in Kantolia had denounced. They were not accused of crimes, as yet. Even the invading army did not yet pretend that they had committed any offense against either military or civilian law. But most of them were frantic. It was not easy to forget tales of hostages shot for acts of resistance by conquered populations. They knew of places where leading citizens had been exterminated for the crime of being leading citizens, and educated men destroyed because they rejected propaganda that outraged all reason. The fate of Kantolia had precedents. If precedent were followed, those first arrested when the land was overrun were in no enviable situation.

Surgeon General Mors tried to reassure them, but he had not much success. The entire situation looked hopeless. The seizure of a single province of a very minor nation would appear to the rest of the world either as a crisis, or an affront to the United Nations, or as a rectification of frontiers – according to the nationality and political persuasion of the commentator. It would go on the agenda of the United Nations Council; deftly it would be intermixed with other matters so that it could not be untangled and considered separately. Ultimately it would be the subject of a compromise – one item in a complicated Great-Power deal – which would leave matters exactly as the invaders wished them. Practically speaking, that was the prospect.

'But the fact,' said Surgeon General Mors, 'is that such

things cannot continue forever. The life of humanity is a symbiosis, a living-together, in all its stages. It begins with the symbiotic relationship of members of a family, each of whom helps and is helped by all the rest. But it rises to the symbiotic relationship of nations, of which each is an organism necessary to the others, and all are mutually helpful.'

'But there is parasitic symbiosis, in which one organism seeks to prey upon another as our enemy seeks to prey upon us,' interjected an amateur naturalist who was a fellow prisoner.

'But a truly healthy organism finds ways to rid itself of parasites,' Mors said calmly; 'or at least to keep them in tolerable subjugation. Do you doubt that our country is a healthy organism?'

It was encouraging talk, but his fellow prisoners were not convinced. Most of them had been seized in their homes. Only one was fully dressed. The mayor had on an overcoat over his nightshirt; his hairy shanks and bare feet left him utterly without dignity. Other leading citizens were unshaven, uncombed and in every possible stage of dishabille; all were certain their humiliation was a bad omen.

'To be sure,' conceded Surgeon General Mors practically, 'our country has only four million people, and our enemy has fifty. But we have planned our nation carefully. In nature, not all creatures defend themselves with tooth and claw. There is a specialized defense for every type of creature, as I myself pointed out to our president. There must be, as I insisted to him, some form of defense for every type of nation, so that it may survive. And I may say that he later told me that he considers our nation's survival certain. So, since this province is necessary if our nation is truly to survive, the invaders will have to be turned out of it.'

'But when?' asked a prisoner despairingly.

'The wheat harvest should begin in three weeks,' said Mors meditatively. 'It will be a great blow to our country if our enemy seizes the wheat harvest. I should say that we must have victory for our country in less than three weeks. Probably within ten days.'

His companions stared at him. But Surgeon General Mors

did not look like someone envisioning a spectacular military triumph for his country. He looked like someone sick at heart from some knowledge he concealed within him.

Depression stayed with the prisoners. They increased in number as the day wore on. Typically, to the conquerors the conquered seemed somehow less than human. Many of the later prisoners had been beaten after their arrest. On the second day the schoolhouse was crowded. More of the new prisoners were beaten. On the third day there was a barbed-wire fence around the schoolhouse and food for the prisoners was contemptuously dumped inside it in bulk for them to distribute themselves. Surgeon General Mors organized a committee for the purpose, and to protest against unnecessary ill-treatment and humiliations.

On the fourth day two men arrived so badly beaten that they were unconscious, and died even as Surgeon General Mors tried – without drugs or any equipment – to revive them.

The newcomers reported conditions in the province. The invaders were methodically looting the captured territory. Their obvious purpose was to increase the riches of their country by impoverishing the province they had added to it. Machinery was being shipped back in a steady stream. Manufactured products were requisitioned from merchants. Kantolia had been the richest province in its small nation. When the invaders finished, it would be the most poverty-stricken in Europe.

That was not all. The troops of the invaders were quartered in private homes as well as in public buildings. Nearly every Kantolian family had its quota of invaders, to be fed at the householder's own expense. And while the enemy troops were required to practice strict discipline in relation to their officers, no such strictness was enforced as regarded civilians. A citizen whose home was only looted was considered fortunate.

The outside world remained unconcerned. Of course no news went out from Kantolia. Censorship and a tightly sealed frontier took care of that. But what sparse, illicit radio news newcomers brought in to the prisoners indicated that the outside world was not too much disturbed by the rectification of an unimportant frontier in a remote corner of Europe.

There was a diplomatic crisis among the Big Four powers. Surgeon General Mors' government had made a dignified protest and a formal appeal to the United Nations, but the achievement of atomic energy control by that organization had been so precarious a matter, and was maintained by so unstable a balance of bargains, that a controversial question like the seizure of Kantolia might wreck the entire framework of international accord if pressed at the present time. Consideration of the matter had been postponed. The invaders had an indefinite period in which forcibly to remold the province's citizenry nearer to their heart's desire, to teach them to clamor dutifully for the maintenance of their new nationality lest worse things befall.

Strangely, though, no new prisoners arrived after the fourth day. Almost the last to arrive told, sobbing, of the fact that fresh troops had been pouring into Kantolia almost from the instant of its seizure, and that now a monstrous army was ready to overwhelm the rest of the nation of which Kantolia had been a part.

But Surgeon General Mors counted on his fingers and said bleakly, 'The invasion cannot last more than ten days! But it is very terrible!'

He had never been military in appearance. Now, five days without soap with which to wash, or a razor with which to shave, and with no change of garments at all, his looks were not imposing. He had torn up his undershirt to make bandages for beaten prisoners. The food was insufficient, and he had given of his own to those most terribly beaten and therefore weakest. The five days had told upon him. Yet he still possessed an odd dignity which could only have been the dignity of faith.

Then, on the afternoon of the fifth day, one of the sentries outside the barbed-wire enclosure staggered, dropped his rifle against a tree and then clung to that tree in a spasm of weakness. And Surgeon General Mors saw it.

He watched somberly until it was over. He looked heartsick and ill. But his eyes glowed doggedly as he turned and ran his eyes over the battered, dispirited figures in the concentration camp which was the first benefit conferred by the invaders.

'I must borrow a razor from someone,' Mors told the mayor of Stadheim, who happened to be nearest him, 'or a knife. At worst I shall have to break a pane of glass and try to shave with its edge. I am going to demand the surrender of the invading army.'

He did not succeed in making the demand that day. It was late afternoon of the seventh day of the occupation before Surgeon General Mors was ushered into the presence of General Vladek. On the way from the schoolhouse, the stocky, untidy man had been marched through the streets of Stadheim. They were almost empty. They were dirty and unswept. Trash littered the sidewalks. He saw few civilians and no soldiers at all except his guard, until he arrived at the capitol building which was enemy headquarters.

He saw an invading soldier there, a sentry, lying on the sidewalk in a curiously shapeless heap. Surgeon General Mors knew at the first glance that the man was dead.

He looked more than ever sick at heart when he was ushered into the presence of General Vladek. The scene of this second interview was also the office of the provincial governor, but now the plebeian elegance of its furnishings had been corrected. Now it was a picture of efficiency. There were filing cabinets and wall maps, and an automatic facsimile machine in one corner hummed softly as it covered a slowly unreeling roll of paper with slightly out-of-register typed orders, queries, lists and the like.

General Vladek was slim and elegantly bemedaled as before. But now there was a nervous tic in his cheek. His face was queerly gray. He looked at Surgeon General Mors with a desperate grimness.

'You are going to be shot,' he said with a terrifying quietness, 'if you answer my questions truthfully. If you do not answer them, you will not be shot. But you will beg very pitifully for a chance to reconsider and earn a firing squad! Do you understand?'

Surgeon General Mors seated himself with great composure. His attempt at shaving had not been very successful. He was in every way a disreputable contrast to the invading general's dapper splendor.

'I asked for this interview,' said Mors matter-of-factly, 'to ask if you are prepared to surrender the troops under your command. You mentioned once that I was the ranking officer of my army in your hands. I doubt that you have captured any other. So I seem to be the person to make the demand.'

General Vladek made a violent gesture. Then he composed himself. But he breathed quickly, and his cheek twitched, and his teeth showed when he smiled. He did not look conspicuously sane.

'What is this epidemic?' he demanded in deadly quietness. 'My men die at the rate of ten thousand a day! Your citizens do not! We have lost thirty-five thousand men in four days, and so far not more than six civilians native to Kantolia have been stricken! *What is it, Mors?*'

Surgeon General Mors leaned back in his chair. He showed no sign of triumph.

'It would be an – organism we developed,' he said heavily. 'The official designation is CK-211. I understand that it is an artificial mutation, a variation on a fairly common bacterium. I have been told that it could be described as a dwarf form of one of the diplococci. It is hardly larger than a virus molecule. You would not expect me to be more precise.'

General Vladek's nostrils distended.

'Ah-h-h-h!' he said with deadly softness. 'It is no normal plague! It is biological war! Too cowardly to fight as honorable men fight, your nation—'

'There is no war between our countries,' said Surgeon General Mors, prosaically, 'and you invaded our country like a brigand, making your own rules for attack. So we made our own rules for defense. If you surrender the troops under your command, there is a good chance that we can save their lives. Have you given thought to the matter?'

General Vladek's cheeks twitched. His hands shook with hate.

'Tell me the truth,' he said hoarsely, 'and I will have you shot. I will concede so much! I promise that I will have you shot! But if you do not—'

'I think you are being absurd, General,' said Mors stolidly. 'As I recall the details, death occurs on the third day after infection, usually within a few hours of the appearance of the first noticeable symptoms. Sulfa, streptomycin, and penicillin are ineffective against this particular strain, which was especially bred up to be resistant to such drugs. Also, from my recollection, the patient is infectious almost from the instant of his own infection. I think you understate your losses. Moreover, in an epidemic of this sort, the death rate should mount geometrically until natural immunes and the lack of susceptibles lower it.'

Mors paused, and said inquiringly, 'You have ordered your men to abstain from all contact with the civil population?'

General Vladek panted with fury.

'I suspected intention when the plague began! My medical corps insisted that since only my men were infected, its cause must be contaminated supplies from home! I ordered my troops to subsist on local supplies and distributed our rations among the people – for revenge in case your spies in our supply system were responsible! But the rate of infection tripled! And your people do not die! My men die! Only my men.'

Surgeon General Mors nodded. His eyes were somber, yet very resolute.

'That is natural,' he observed. 'Our population is immune.' Then he said explanatorily. 'We have immunized practically our entire population against certain formerly prevalent diseases. And included in the injection given to each citizen was a fraction of a very interesting formula which produces immunity to diplococci in a quite new fashion.'

The dapper General Vladek sat frozen and speechless, in a rage so murderous that he seemed almost calm.

'It makes symbiosis possible,' said Surgeon General Mors, in an interested tone. 'It produces a condition under which the human body and the entire series of diplococci can live together. It does not produce the relationship. That requires the organisms, too. It merely makes the relationship possible. We have had practically no diplococci infections in our country for years back. Such diseases happen to be very rare among us. But the inoculation makes it possible for any of our inoculated citizens to establish a truly symbiotic relationship in case he encounters them. It is like the adjustment of intestinal flora and colon bacilli to us. They do not harm us, and we do not harm them. You follow the reasoning?'

General Vladek's voice was quite inhuman. 'How were my men infected?' he demanded. His voice cracked. 'Tell me, how were my men infected? My medical corps says—'

'We did not infect them,' said Surgeon General Mors calmly. 'We infected only our own population. On the morning of your invasion we spread the infection in the drinking water, in the food. We infected our own people – who could not be harmed by it – and then I came to you and warned you to keep your soldiers aloof from our people. I also advised you to get your troops out of our country for their own safety, but you would not believe me. Because you see' – his tone was absolutely commonplace – 'every citizen of our country is now a carrier of the plague of which your soldiers die. A carrier. Not suffering from it, but able to give it to anyone not immunized against it. You have heard of typhoid carriers. We are a nation of carriers, bearers of the plague which is destroying your army.'

General Vladek looked like an image of frozen, despairing rage. His face was gray. His cheek twitched. He had led an invading army triumphantly into this province.

Then without one shot being fired, his army had ceased to be an army, and a sentry lay dead on the street before his headquarters.

'We did not like to do it,' said Surgeon General Mors, heavily. 'But we had to defend ourselves. The soil of our nation is now deadly to your troops. If you murdered and burned every citizen of our country, our land would still be fatal to your men and to the settlers who might follow them. You cannot make use of Kantolia. You cannot make use of any of the rest of our country. And the loot you have sent back has spread infection in your cities. Couriers have carried it back and transmitted it before they died. The quislings you sent to your country to be rewarded for betraying their own – they were carriers, too. The plague must rage horribly in your nation. Other countries will close their frontiers in quarantine, if they have not already done so. Your nation is destroyed unless you let us save it. I beg that you will give us the power.'

Then Surgeon General Mors said very wearily: 'I hope you will surrender your army, General Vladek. Your men, as our prisoners, will become our patients and we will cure them. Otherwise they will die. Permit us, and we will check the epidemic you created in your own country by invading us. We did not defend ourselves without knowing our weapon thoroughly. But you will have to give us the power to rescue you. You and your nation must surrender without conditions. . . .'

General Vladek stood up. He rang a bell. An officer and soldiers entered.

'Take him out,' panted General Vladek hoarsely. Then his voice rose to a scream. 'Take him out and kill him!'

The officer moved. Then there was a clatter. A rifle had dropped to the floor. One of the soldiers staggered. He reeled against one of the steel filing cases and clung there desperately. Sweat poured out on his face; he was ashen white. He knew, of course, what was the matter. He sobbed. He was already a dead man, though he still moved and breathed. Great tears welled out of his eyes.

The other soldiers wavered – and fled.

Surgeon General Mors stood beside a pigsty and argued patiently with a peasant who so far had stubbornly refused to permit the reinoculation of either his family or his cows. The dumpy little man in the badly fitting uniform said earnestly:

'It is a matter of living together – what learned men call symbiosis. We defended our country with the other inoculations. Now we must defend all mankind with these! We do not want our people to be feared or hated. We want visitors from other nations to come and live among us in peace and safety, to have no fears about doing business with us. If other nations are afraid of us, we will suffer for it!'

The peasant made fitful objections. Victory over the invaders, and the terms imposed upon them, had made him proud. But Surgeon General Mors' patient arguments were gradually wearing him down.

'Ah, but they made war on us. That was different! We do not want any more wars. When you and your family and your cows have been inoculated, we will be that much further along toward the understanding that nations which are at peace can live together,' said Surgeon General Mors earnestly. 'Nations which are at war only die together.'

INTERFERENCE

Time travel. A theme that fascinated Leinster, who made it the subject of a number of short stories. A collection of his stories on this theme appeared about sixteen years ago, and it was obvious that Leinster was aware of the paradoxes involved. Some of his 'solutions' were ingenious in the extreme. In the present story it is the results, rather than the mechanics, of the operation, that are considered.

THE racket came on the air about eight o'clock, and at eight-five the business office of American Broadcasting went up in the air like a gyrocket, making similar shrill screaming noises. The row came from somewhere in Brooklyn, and there wasn't a vision set in thirty miles – fifteen million customers – that could get anything but crazy streaks on its plate, or anything but a steady rasping noise on audio. It was just before the Melba Hour when Little Angy went on the air, and Little Angy was something the customers couldn't do without. So when this noise started on the vision channels at this special time, the business office began to shriek and wring its hands, and every locator-car on the prowl went streaking.

The racket wasn't too hard to locate. Of course, like all short stuff, we had to chase it around corners. Mort and me, we went around one block three times before Mort realized that the whole block was one big warehouse and it had aluminum-foil insulation which was batting the stuff back and forth with a couple of fire-walls and vertical metal signs elsewhere. When we made a bigger circuit around it, we got back on the line and only had to track off three places where it was coming from two directions at once, and one where there were three steady beams of it from as many casual reflectors. But it didn't help any that the business office was having hysterics on the car set, telling us that Little Angy would be going on in twenty minutes, in fifteen minutes, that there were already two thousand complaints, the mayor had called up to find out what was the matter and the Pinky-Pank company had already filed a penalty-claim on the ground of loss of coverage, and if something wasn't done quick— And so on.

We found it, though. The stuff was coming out of a block of dingy-looking buildings, some of them occupied tenements and some boarded up. It was a pretty bum neighborhood. What always makes it worse is that when you get close enough to short stuff with power behind it, it's bouncing off every pot and kettle and gives you secondary dispersion-beams. So Mort and me, we piled out of our car and were just starting to work when the other cars came, and we divided up the street. We got started banging on doors with the old line of excuse-me-lady-but - there's - some - electrical - device - making - television - wavelength - interference - in - this - neighborhood - do - you - know - anybody - who - does - electrical - experimenting - and - so - on. It ain't scientific, but it's usually pretty quick. Meanwhile we had our hand-receivers and were using them frantic. *And* the business office was throwing fits.

Mort ran into a fighting drunk who answered his door and wanted to put up an argument, and I was yelling in a deaf woman's ear when my hand-receiver got the line; plain and clear, no out-of-phase stuff, all regular, polarized beam. I yelled to Mort. It was next door to the house where we were so we dusted down into the street. Next door was boarded up, and so was the house beyond, so we hauled off some planks and smashed a window and shinnied in, leaving one guy outside to explain to cops if any. Inside, we heard a soft sort of humming sound and we streaked it up the stairs – because Little Angy would be coming on in ten minutes or less, now – and I saw a sort of glow coming outa a door and I ran there, yelling:

'Hey, guy! Turn it off! Whatever it is, turn it off!'

And I went to the door to argue further, with Mort and three other guys from the other locator-cars behind me. And there it was.

Nope. No dead man. Not yet. The dead man came later. What we saw when we went in was a four-foot kinda ring of light hanging about a foot under the ceiling. It was a pinkish-bluish light, reasonably bright – you could read by it easy enough – and humming softly to itself. But the thing was that it wasn't in a tube. It wasn't hanging on to anything. It was just there, absolutely still and absolutely solid. It looked like a ring of something that – well – it looked more like a ring of red-hot glass than anything else, if you get what I mean. Only there wasn't any heat and it was just bright regardless, there in midair. And it was still as if it had angle irons and braces holding it. It was fixed in place somehow! But you couldn't see how.

Mort stared at it, and the other guys too. Then Mort said:

'This is it, whatever it is. How do you turn it off?'

'Little Angy's coming on in five minutes,' says another guy, to whom the business office was the law and the prophets. 'We got to do something! We got to turn it off!'

'Sure!' I said. I'd been prowling around it, looking at it from every angle there was. 'Show me a switch or a wire. This is a job for somebody who knows more than I do.'

We all stared at it. It didn't move. It was solid! Then Mort said:

'No wires, no switch, no nothing. We gotta get some foil and beam it up. Let Tech figure it out. Any of you fellas wants to touch it, go ahead. I'm gonna beam it!'

He went out. A couple of the other fellas went with him. I heard 'em running downstairs. They were using flashlights. I heard the crash when they broke out the front door. We rate as emergency maintenance crews, you know, so it's not burglary or trespassing when we go barging around, any more than firemen or cops.

I fiddled with my hand-receiver. Yep, that was it. The stuff that was messing up all the television reception in the whole metrop was that ring of stuff hanging up there like a brick wall. There wasn't any wire to it, but it was radiating a flock of kilowatts. Mort came racing back with a big roll of paper-backed metal foil and some tape. The other fellas came with folding ladders. We got busy. It's funny, but nobody thought of touching it, or socking it with something, or trying to short it to a burn-out. It was too simple. Mort hung a sheet of foil to the ceiling, sticking it up with adhesive tape here and there. He strung it a yard from the ring. Another fella was setting up another one. They hung down like curtains, opposite each other. We stuck up two more, working fast. We had a kinda curtain around it, then. Then we swung the bottom edges of the metal-foil curtains toward each other so there was part of a sort of four-sided funnel around the thing. The short stuff it was giving off bounced off the foil and went straight up, and stuff like that goes straight through the heaviside layer. One fella went down to his car and came back.

'Business office says sets are workin' again,' he reported. 'Now we got to hunt for strays.'

You don't often beam off interference, you know. Anything but a power line you usually turn off, firm, and let the legal department argue about it after. But if and when a power line has a leak that's making television-type interference, you beam it off like we'd done to this thing. It don't happen once in a coon's age, but we know how to do it. And we'd done it in time for Little Angy to go on the air and be received by an amusement-hungry populace.

O.K. We started looking for stray leakages of short stuff. We used more foil. Then Mort reported in, and all the check stations said O.K., and Mort came back and said:

'Buck and me have to sit by the fire till Tech gets here. Scram, you fellas.'

The other fellas went out. There was some interference up in the Bronx. Four blocks hadn't any service at all, and the image was wabbling beyond that. So one car went there to find out who was using an ultraviolet machine with a bum condenser in it, and the others went on the prowl. Mort and me settled down for a rest. But when the others were gone, Mort looked at me with a kinda triumphant expression in his eyes.

'Buck,' he says. 'Whadda you think this thing is?'

'I've got three headaches already,' I told him, 'trying to figure it out.'

'I got a hunch,' he says again. 'Did you ever hear of time travel?'

Sure! But it ain't possible. There was a guy proved that if you could travel in time you'd have to pass through all the time in between where you started from and where you went, and passing through meant being there, so you'd have to be spread out through all the time in between. And if you were spread out over a coupla hundred years it would be the same thing as being spread out over a coupla hundred miles. Not practical. Anyhow, not healthy. I said so.

'O.K.,' says Mort, 'but I've got a hunch you're seeing a time-travel device. Nobody on this earth at this time could make a thing like that. So it must be somebody at another time. Notice you can't look through the ring?'

I squinted up at it, and it was so. You could see the ceiling past the edge of the ring, and when we were hanging up the foil we saw the ceiling over the top of it. But I couldn't look through the ring of light.

'It's a doorway,' says Mort. 'Perhaps we'd better say a sort of elevator shaft to the future. It's a way so somebody maybe a hundred thousand years in the future can come back and look us over.'

I felt funnier the longer I stayed around that ring of light. At first I'd been too busy trying to figure out how to handle the short stuff it was giving off, but now that we didn't have anything to do but wait for Tech to send somebody – and they'd take their time – I began to think that it was something very queer indeed.

'Yeah?' I said. 'It's a way for somebody to come from another time, huh? Well then, where is he?'

The house we were in was all boarded up. We hadn't seen or heard anything at all, only noises we'd made ourselves.

'M-m-m,' says Mort. 'That's right. Let's look.'

We'd come along a hallway to this room from the stairs. But

there was another door inside here, and it was open. All the place was empty and old, with plaster falling down and everything dilapidated and dusty and musty-smelling. Mort took out his flashlight and went through that other door, swinging the beam around. He's hardly through when he lets out a squawk. Then there's silence, like he might've had to swallow to get so he could talk. Then:

'He's here,' says Mort, strained. 'He's right here. You might come see.'

I felt cold chills run down my back. Mort says again:

'He's dead.'

I went in and saw the dead man. He laid down on the floor, in the dust that was everywhere. He was a regular-looking guy, not any different from you or me, except his face had a funny expression on it. Some of the guys in Tech have that expression – the high-ups, mostly. College professors have it pretty often – not the higher-ups. Most chemists and a lot of preachers have it. It's the expression of a guy who doesn't worry about beating the other guy to something because he's busy with stuff more important to him than that. A sort of non-competitive look, you might say. The average guy on salary has not got it.

He laid there, stone dead, just where he'd dropped. There wasn't a mark on him. He seemed to be dressed just like you and me, the first instant you looked at him. But he wasn't. The cloth was different. His clothes weren't cut exactly right. And his shoes – Mort said:

'Look at those shoes, willya?'

They weren't leather, but something else. They were made to look sort of like our shoes, but they were one piece. They weren't put together. They were – well molded, maybe. The same thing with his clothes. They weren't sewed together. They were just made. This stuff turned up later, you understand, and I found it out when Mort and me were being driven crazy by professors and such trying to drag more information out of us than we had. But right at the beginning I saw that this guy woulda looked perfectly all right if you just glanced at him casual, but if you looked close you'd see the difference. But he was a pleasant-faced fella, at that.

'What—' I swallowed. 'What killed 'im?'

'I dunno,' says Mort. 'I guess the cops will be askin' us that presently. So I'm goin' to take a look, first.'

He fished in the fella's pockets. They weren't right. Mort's arm went in almost up to the elbow. He came out with a handful of stuff. He handed half of it to me and stared at the rest. That was when I first saw the picture of the girl. I almost dropped when I first looked at it, because it didn't look like a flat picture. It looked like I was looking in through a window at some scenery that went on forever. Three-dimensional stuff, you know. But was it three-dimensional? There was light behind the girl, and it was sure-enough light behind her. And that girl looked sweet. Like a darned sweet kid. A little bit wistful, but confident and brave and smiling and looking at somebody she liked a lot. Maybe – I figured this out later, too – the guy who'd had the picture had taken it, and she smiled at him while he was doing it. I'd like to have a girl like that smile at me like that.

I was staring at the picture when Mort swore:

'What,' he says, 'is this stuff for?'

There was a thing like three or four rings interlocked, only they couldn't move but so far in any direction. What it was for is your guess, I don't know. There was a little card with a sort of stubby pencil. Later on we found out there are all sorts of coils and condensers and things inside the thickness of the card, all packed in so it's no thicker than it needs to be for you to hold it. Somebody has figured since that it's a sort of recording telegraph, so you can send a written message to somebody at a distance, but nobody can make it work, yet. And there was a thing that looked like a cigarette lighter, with a thumb stud. Mort pushed it and a streak of blue light came out and there was a small round hole up to the sky. Then his hand jumped, and the round hole changed to a wavery empty space like a saw-cut through the ceiling and roof and everything.

Mort dropped it, and his face went white.

'Let's get out of here!' says Mort.

We went back in the room with the light. Mort was white as a sheet, but suddenly he says:

'That proves it! It's a time-travelin' device. We couldn't make things like this. This guy came from some place a million years from now!'

I shoved the picture in my pocket and showed him the rest of what I had. There was a little ball of white metal. Period. There was a flat white square of something that looked like plastic. Period. There was a bit of machinery that was working. You could see wheels like clockworks running inside of a glass-like case. It didn't make sense.

'This guy musta been crazy,' I said, trying to pretend I wasn't dizzy inside. 'What does a grown man want to carry marbles and ring-puzzles and funny-shaped blocks of plastic for? And what does he carry machinery like this, for?'

'We carry watches,' says Mort. He added, his eyes gleaming. 'Look! This guy came back to our time from a million years A.D.'

'He ain't bald and he's got teeth,' I said, objecting. 'He looks just like you and me.'

'Maybe not a million,' says Mort, feverish. 'Maybe fifty thousand. Maybe only twenty-five thousand. But our civilization's only a coupla thousand years old. The electric part's not two hundred, yet! Suppose a guy like you went back a hundred thousand years and a cave man went through your pockets. You've got a pocketknife. He'd never get it open. You've got a watch. He'd never guess there was such a thing as hours and minutes. Your fountain pen – what'd he know of writing? Your little black book wouldn't mean a thing to him. Your handkerchief— He'd never guess what it was for. What have you got that he'd understand? Gum? Matches? Tobacco? Money? See what I mean?'

I said:

'There's a dead man in there, and we'd better call the cops and tell 'em.'

'Not yet!' says Mort. His eyes glittered and blinked. He trembled all over. 'Look here, Buck! This guy came from the future. There's no doubt about it ! The door he came through is still right there! If that door's still open, guys from the technical department will get to talking through it when they come. They'll all get credit and all the benefit outa it. But if we can get some information ahead of those guys we can clean up! Think what they must have in the future that we ain't got! Their television sets oughta be honeys. Their—'

He shook all over. Mort is a pretty smart guy in some ways, but he didn't see the real point he'd just made. To tell the truth, neither did I. I've got a developing set and a printer, though, and I take a lot of pictures. So I could see – I'd already seen that if I could dope out how that three-dimensional stuff was done I'd really have something. So I was willing to go along with Mort for a while.

'What're you going to do?' I asked.

Mort already had his wallet out. He had his driver's license out from behind its celluloid window. His hand trembled.

'I'm goin' to do a card trick,' says Mort. But his voice shook.

He took his driver's license and skimmed it up at the center of the ring of light. It went right through. It shoulda hit the ceiling and dropped back. It didn't. If it had fallen anywhere but back through the ring, it woulda hit the foil and come back to the floor anyway. But it just vanished.

'They've got it,' says Mort, shivering. 'They've got my picture and my driver's license. That's to tell 'em somebody else besides the guy in the next room is trying to talk to 'em. Maybe English has changed so much they can't read our kind a hundred thousand years from now. Anyhow—'

He tossed up a quarter. Hard. If it had hit the ceiling, we'd have heard it. The light ring didn't hum too loud for that. But the quarter went through the middle of the ring that we couldn't see through, and it didn't hit anything, and it didn't drop back.

'Gimme something to throw through!' say Mort. 'So they'll understand what I'm trying to do!'

He took an envelope out of his pocket and scribbled on it: '*Hello! Hello! Hello! Men of the future, hello!*' He skimmed it up. It didn't come back either.

Then he sat there, biting his nails, staring up. So did I. And then something came down out of the middle of the ring of light. It was a metal rod with a round glass ball on the end of it. It came down, stayed for maybe a second, and went up again.

'There wasn't any hole in the ceiling!' says Mort, his teeth chattering. 'What was that? What would we do if we were on the other side of a ring like that—'

I said maybe the only intelligent thing I thought of during the whole business.

'If we were working on it from that end,' I said, 'and we wanted to know what happened to a guy we were scared to follow, we'd shove a camera through to snap his picture.'

'Right!' says Mort, staring at me. 'Now they'll see us an' know we're trying to talk to 'em—'

We waited. The rod came down again. It had a clamp on the end of it now. There was a picture in the clamp. It was a picture of the guy who was dead in the next room.

'They want to know where he is!' said Mort.

He took the picture out of the clamp. He was so excited that he didn't notice what I saw right away. That picture was three-dimensional color, too. It stood out just like the picture of the girl I had in my pocket. But Mort took it, and on the blank back side of it he scribbled a sketch of a man lying down on the floor – it was a bum picture – with two other men standing by him. And he drew the two other men, who were supposed to be us, looking very sad and grief-stricken.

He put it back in the clamp and shoved it up. It went on up through the ring. There was a long pause. Mort got restless.

'I'm not a good artist,' he said shakily. 'Maybe they think we killed him. Say! I'm going to send up my hand-receiver.'

He picked it up and tossed it through the ring of light. It stayed gone, though I couldn't help wincing and waiting to hear it crash. But it didn't. It stayed put.

Then the clamp came down once more. It had another picture in it. At least, it had a sheet of paper that seemed to be all black on one side. But when Mort grabbed it and looked at it, it seemed to be all dancing spots of light. He tore his hair.

'I don't get it!' he says, feverish. 'I send 'em my picture and they send a camera down. Then they send a picture of the dead guy in the next room. I send 'em up a handset, that'll at least show 'em we can handle short waves, and they send me a picture with a lot of sparkles on it.'

I stared at the picture. The sparkles were different sizes and tints. Suddenly I saw it.

'This's a star map!' I said. 'Look! It's a picture of the sky! There's the Big Dipper! See? And there's the Little Dipper and the Pole Star! But what's it for?'

Mort fairly yelled with relief.

'I got it!' he panted. 'They figured out! If we send 'em a picture of the stars, they can figure out if they hit the time they were aiming for! They're askin' us what year this is!'

He ran out of the room and downstairs. I knew what he was after. He used to read those popular science magazines, and they always have a star map in them, telling amateur astronomers where to find planets and comets and such. He had one of them in the locator-car. He'd gone after it.

I waited. The clamp hung down. There was a dead man in the next room. Presently I figured maybe they'd get tired of waiting, so I tore a leaf out of my little black book and drew the clamp, and then another picture. It was a stick-man running downstairs. Then I drew him taking something out of a car, and then running upstairs again. I put it in the clamp and gave it a shove and it was pulled up and vanished. And they understood all right. The clamp came down again, empty, and it waited.

I was looking at the picture of the girl when I heard Mort on his way upstairs again.

'I got it!' he panted. 'Here's this magazine and I've opened to the star map for this month. They'll realize we got sense and we'll learn plenty!'

He tied a string about the magazine where it was already opened, and put it in the clamp. He shoved it, and it went up. Mort stood there, staring feverishly, figuring what he was going to ask next. The star map stayed up there. The clamp didn't come down. Nothing happened.

Then the ring of light went out. And it stayed out.

Mort tore out most of his hair when the thing stayed that way. He might have gone off his nut if a smart scientist from a research foundation hadn't talked confidentially to both of us a few days later.

'Nobody in the world coulda done better,' said that guy comfortingly. 'They were trying time travel, and the math is tricky. They wanted to find out if they'd gone into the future or the past. You told them with that star map – neither – and they went away. There's nothing here they wanted. We're like cave men, to them. Nothing we could say would interest 'em. You did all right.'

Mort said:

'But – listen! Where did they come from? And that dead guy—'

'What does it matter where they came from?' asked the guy from the foundation. 'A parallel time track most likely, where they got started up the ladder say fifty thousand years before us. But the important thing is what we get out of it. And we get plenty. Those gadgets. That dead man – we know he got killed because he didn't wear an insulated suit when he came through that ring. Since he didn't, he lived only five minutes. But when *we* go barging around in time we'll know how to do it.'

I'd been listening, and I butted in:

'Yeah,' I said, 'you think we're going to do that sort of thing too? You guess we'll go – well – to where those guys came from?'

'Why not?' says the guy from the foundation. 'In a thousand years?'

It was ten days after the whole business began. I'd had a lot of time to think.

'Listen,' I said, 'when you get set and you want somebody to wear an insulated suit, you let me know, huh?'

I grinned, but I've still got that picture the dead guy had on him. It's a picture of a swell kid. A darned sweet kid. And somehow I don't feel like grinning when I think of it. I wouldn't mind trying to find that kid to give her back her picture and tell her I'm sorry about the guy.

DE PROFUNDIS

Monsters. A story written more than 25 years ago. At that time plot was still usually considered of more importance than character development, particularly in an alien; it would take Hal Clement (Needle, Iceworld, A Matter of Gravity) *to force SF readers to accept that aliens, too, were only human. Nevertheless, the degree of identification with the narrator of the following story is considerable, bearing in mind that he/she/it is literally a veritable B.E.M.!*

I, SARD, make report to the Shadi during Peace Tides. I have made a journey of experiment suggested by the scientist Morpt after discussing with me an Object fallen into Honda from the Surface. I fear that my report will not be accepted as true. I therefore await the consensus on my sanity, offering this report to be judged science or delirium as the Shadi may elect....

I was present when the Object fell. At the moment I was in communication with the scientist Morpt as he meditated upon the facts of the universe. He was rather drowsy, and his mind was more conscientious than inspiring as he reflected – for the benefit of us, his students – upon the evidence of the Caluphian theory of the universe, that it is a shell of solid matter filled with water, which being naturally repelled from the centre, acquires pressure, and that we, the Shadi, live in the region of greatest pressure. He almost dozed off as he reflected for our instruction that this theory accounts for all known physical phenomena, except the existence of the substance gas, which is neither solid nor liquid and is found only in our swim-bladders. For this reason, it is commonly assumed to be our immortal part, rising to the center of the universe when our bodies are consumed, and there exists forever.

As he meditated, I recalled the Morpt exercises by which a part of this gas may be ejected from a Shadi body and kept in an inverted receptacle while the body forms a new supply in the swim-bladder. I waited anxiously for Morpt's trenchant reasoning which denies that a substance – however rare and singular – which can be kept in a receptacle or replaced by the body can constitute its vital essence.

These experiments of Morpt's have caused great disturbances among scientific circles.

At the moment, however, he was merely a drowsy instructor, sleepily thinking a lecture he had thought a hundred times before. He was a little annoyed by a sharp rock sticking into his seventh tentacle, which was not quite uncomfortable enough to make him stir.

I lay in my cave, attending anxiously. Then, abruptly, I was aware that something was descending from above. The instinct of our race to block out thought-transference and seize food before any one else can know of it, operated instantly. I flowed out of my cave and swept to the space below the Object. I raised my tentacles to snatch it. The whole process was automatic – mind-block on, spatial sensation extended to the fullest, full focused reception of mental images turned upon the sinking Object to foresee its efforts to escape so that I could anticipate them – but every Shadi knows what one does by pure instinct when a moving thing comes within one's ken.

There were two causes for my behavior after that automatic reaction, however. One was that I had fed, and lately. The other was that I received mental images from within the Object which were startlingly tuned to the subject of Morpt's lecture and my own thoughts of the moment. As my first tentacle swooped upon the descending thing, instead of thoughts of fright or battle, I intercepted the message of an entity, cogitating despairingly, to another.

'My dear, we will never see the Surface again,' it was thinking.

And I received a dazzling impression of what the Surface was like. Since I shall describe the Surface later, I omit a description of the mental picture I then received. But it gave me to pause, I believe fortunately. For one thing, had I swept the Object into my maw as instinct impelled, I believe I would have had trouble digesting it. The Object, as I soon discovered, was made of that rare solid substance which only appears in the form of artifacts. One such specimen has been repeatedly described by Glor. It is about half the length of a Shadi's body, hollow, pointed at one end, with one of its sides curiously flat with strangely shaped excrescences, openings, and two shafts and one hollow tube sticking out of it.

As I said, the Object was made of this rare solid material. My spatial sense immediately told me that it was hollow. Further, that it was filled with gas! And then I received conflicting mental images which told me that there were two living creatures within it! Let me repeat – there were two living entities within the Object, and they lived in gas instead of water!

I was stunned. For a long time I was not really aware of anything at all save the thoughts of the creatures within the Object. I held the Object firmly between two of my tentacles, dazed by the impossible facts I faced. I was most incautious. I could have been killed and consumed in the interval of my bewilderment. But I came to myself and returned swiftly to my cave, carrying the Object with me. As I did so, I was aware of startled thoughts.

'We've hit bottom – no! Something has seized us. It must be monstrous in size. It will soon be over, now. . . .'

Not in answer, but separately, the other entity thought only emotional things I cannot describe. I do not understand them at all. They represent a psychology so alien to ours that there is no way to express them. I can only say that the second entity was in complete despair, and therefore desired intensely to be clasped firmly in the other entity's two tentacles. This would constitute complete helplessness, but it was what the second creature craved. I report the matter with no attempt to explain it.

'While flowing into my cave, I knocked the Object against

the top of the opening. It was a sharp blow. I had again an impression of despair.

'This is it!' the first creature thought, and looked with dread for an inpouring of water into the gas-filled Object.

Since the psychology of these creatures is so completely inexplicable, I merely summarize the few mental images I received during the next short period which served to explain the history of the Object.

To begin with, it had been a scientific experiment. The Object was created to contain the gas in which the creatures lived, and to allow the gas to be lowered into the regions of pressure. The creatures themselves were of the same species, but different in a fashion for which we have no thought. One thought of itself as 'man', the other as 'woman'. They did not fear each other. They had accompanied the Object for the purpose of recording their observations in regions of pressure. To make their observations, the Object was suspended by a long tentacle from an artifact like the one of Glor's description.

When they had observed, they were to have been returned to the artifact. Then the gas was to be released, and they would rejoin their fellows. The fact that two creatures could remain together with safety for both is strange enough. But their thoughts told me that forty or fifty others of the same species awaited then on the artifact, all equally devoid of the instinct to feed upon each other.

This appears impossible, of course, and I merely report the thought-images I received. However, while at the full length of the tentacle which held it, the tentacle broke. The Object therefore sank down into the regions of pressure in which we Shadi live. As it neared solidity, I reached up and grasped it and miraculously did not swallow it. I could have done so with ease.

When, in my cave, I had attended for some time to the thoughts coming from within the Object, I tried to communicate. First, of course, I attempted to paralyze the creatures with fear. They did not seem to be aware of the presence of mind. I then attempted, more gently, to converse with them.

But they seemed to be devoid of the receptive faculty. They are rational creatures, but even with no mind-block up, they are completely unaware of the thoughts of others. In fact, their thoughts were plainly secret from each other.

I tried to understand all this, and failed. At long last a proper humility came to me, and I sent out a mental call to Morpt. He was still drowsily detailing the consequences of the Caluph theory – that in the center of the universe the gas which has escaped from the swim-bladders of dead Shadi has gathered to form a vast bubble, and that the border between the central bubble and the water is the legendary Surface.

Legends of the Surface are well-known. Morpt reflected, in sleepy irony, that if gas is the immortal part of Shadi, then since two Shadi who see each other instantly fight to the death, the bubble at the center of the universe must be the scene of magnificent combat. But his irony was lost upon me. I interrupted to tell him of the Object and what I had already learned from it.

I immediately felt other minds crowd me. All of Morpt's pupils were instantly alert. I blanked out my mind with more than usual care – to avoid giving any clue to the whereabouts of my cave – and served science to the best of my ability. I told, freely, everything I knew.

Under other conditions, I would have been proud of the furor I created. It seemed that every Shadi in the Honda joined the discussion. Many, of course, said that I lied. But I was fed, and filled with curiosity. I did not reveal my whereabouts to those challengers. I waited. Even Morpt tried to taunt me into an incautious revelation and went into a typical Shadi rage when he failed. But Morpt is experienced and huge. I could not hope to be the one to live did we meet each other outside of the Peace Tides.

Once I had proved I could not be lured out, however, Morpt discussed the matter dispassionately and in the end suggested the journey from which I have just returned. If, despite my caution where other Shadi were concerned – all of Morpt's pupils will recognize the challenging irony with which he thought this – if, despite my caution, I was not afraid to serve science, he advised me to carry the Object back to the Heights. From the creatures within it I should receive directions. From their kind I had my strength and ferocity as protections. From the Heights, themselves, Morpt urged his exercises as the only possible safeguards.

As I knew, said Morpt, the gas in our swim-bladders expands as pressure lessens. Normally, we have muscles which control it so that we can float in pursuit of our prey or sink to solidity at will. But he told me that as I neared the Heights I would find the pressure growing so small that in theory even my muscles would be unable to control the gas. Under such conditions I must use the Morpt exercises and release a portion of it. Then I could descend again.

Otherwise, I might actually be carried up by my own expanding gas, it might rupture my swim-bladder and invade other body cavities and expand still further, and finally carry me with it up to the Surface and the central bubble of Caluph's theory.

In such a case, Morpt assured me wittily, I would become one Shadi who knew whether Caluph was right or not, but I would not be likely to return to tell about it. Still, he insisted, if I paused to use his exercises whenever I felt unusually buoyant, I would certainly carry the Object quite near the Surface without danger and so bring back conclusive evidence of the truth or error of the entire Caluphian cosmology, thus rendering a great service to science. The thoughts coming from within the Object should be of great assistance in the enterprise.

I immediately determined to make the journey. For one thing, I was not too sure that I could keep my whereabouts hidden, if continually probed by older and more experienced minds. Only exceedingly powerful minds, like those of Morpt and the other instructors, can risk exposure to constant hungry inspection. Of course, they find the profit in their instructorships in such slips among their students....

It would be distinctly wise for me to leave my cave, now that I had called attention to myself. So I put up my mind-block tightly and with the Object clutched in one tentacle, I flowed swiftly up the slope which surrounds Honda before other Shadi should think of patrolling it for me – and each other.

I went far above my usual level before I paused. I went so high that the gas in my swim-bladder was markedly uncomfortable. I did the Morpt exercises until it was released. It was strange that I did this with complete calm. But my curiosity was involved now, and we Shadi are inveterate seekers. So I found it possible to perform an act – the deliberate freeing of a part of the contents of my swim-bladder – which would have filled past generations of Shadi with horror.

Morpt was right. I was able to continue my ascent without discomfort. More, with increasing Height, I had much for my mind to think of. The two creatures – the man and the woman – in the Object were bewildered by what had happened to their container.

'We have risen two thousand feet from our greatest depth,' the man said to the woman.

'My dear, you don't have to lie to make me brave,' the woman said. 'I don't mind. I couldn't have kept you out of the bathysphere, and I'd rather die with you than live without you.'

Such thoughts do not seem compatible with intelligence. A race with such a psychology would die out. But I do not pretend to understand.

I continued upward until it was necessary to perform the Morpt exercises again. The necessary movements shook the Object violently. The creatures within speculated hopelessly upon the cause. These creatures not only lack the receptive faculty, so that their thoughts are secret from each other, but apparently they have no spatial sense, no sense of pressure and apparently fail of the cycle of instincts which is so necessary to us Shadi.

In all the time of my contact with their minds, I found no thought of anything approximating the Peace Tides, when we Shadi cease altogether to feed and, therefore, instinctively cease to fear each other and intermingle freely to breed. One wonders how their race can continue without Peace Tides, unless their whole lives are passed in a sort of Peace Tide. In that case, since no one feeds during the Peace Tides, why are they not starved to death? They are inexplicable.

They watched their instruments as the ascent went on. Instruments are artifacts which they use to supplement their defective senses.

'Four thousand feet up,' said the man to the woman. 'Only heaven knows what has happened!'

'Do you think there's a chance for us?' the woman said yearningly.

'How could there be?' the man demanded bitterly. 'We sank to eighteen thousand feet. There is still almost three miles of water over our heads, and the oxygen won't last forever. I wish I hadn't let you come. If only you were safe!'

Four thousand feet – whatever that term may mean – above the Honda, the character of living things had changed. All forms of life were smaller, and their spatial sense seemed imperfect. They were not aware of my coming until I was actually upon them. I kept two tentacles busy snatching them as I passed. Their body lights were less brilliant than those of the lesser creatures of the Honda.

I continued my flowing climb toward the Surface. From time to time, I paused to perform the Morpt exercises. The volume of gas I released from my swim-bladder was amazing. I remember thinking, in somewhat the ironic manner of Morpt himself, that if ever Shadi possessed so vast an immortal part, the central bubble must be greater than Honda itself! The creatures inside the Object now watched their instruments incredulously.

'We are up to nine thousand feet,' said the man dazedly. 'We dropped to eighteen thousand, the greatest depth in this part of the world.'

The thought 'world' approximates the Shadi conception of 'universe', but there are puzzling differences.

'We've risen half of it again,' the man added.

'Do you think that the ballast dropped off and we will float to the Surface?' asked the woman anxiously.

The thought of 'ballast' was of things fastened to the Object to make it descend, and that if they were detached, the Object would rise. This would seem to be nonsense, because all substances descend, except gas. However, I report only what I sensed.

'But we're not floating,' said the man. 'If we were, we'd rise steadily. As it is, we go up a thousand feet or so and then we're practically shaken to death. Then we go up another thousand feet. We're not floating. We're being carried. But only the fates know by what or why.'

This, I point out, is rationality. They knew that their rise was unreasonable. My curiosity increased. I should explain how the creatures knew of their position. They have no spatial sense or any sense of pressure. For the latter they used instruments – artifacts – which told of their ascent. The remarkable thing is that they inspected those instruments by means of a light which they did not make themselves. The light was also made by an artifact. And this artificial light was strong enough to be reflected, not only perceptibly, but distinctly, so that the instruments were seen by reflection only.

I fear that Kanth, whose discovery that light is capable of reflection made his scientific reputation, will deny that any light could be powerful enough to make unlighted objects appear to have light, but I must go even further. As I learned to share not only consciously formed thoughts but sense-impressions of the creatures in the Object, I learned that to them, light has different qualities. Some lights have qualities which to them are different from other lights.

The light we know they speak of as 'bluish'. They know additional words which they term 'red' and 'white' and 'yellow' and other terms. As we perceive difference in the solidity of rocks and ooze, they perceive differences in objects by the light they reflect. Thus, they have a sense which we Shadi have not. I am aware that Shadi are the highest possible type of organism, but this observation – if not insanity – is important matter for meditation.

But I continued to flow steadily upward, pausing only to perform the necessary Morpt exercises to release gas from my swim-bladder when its expansion threatened to become uncontrollable. As I went higher and ever higher, the man and woman were filled with emotions of a quite extraordinary nature. These emotions were unbearably poignant to them, and it is to be doubted that any Shadi has ever sensed such sensations before. Certainly the emotion they call 'love' is inconceivable to Shadi, except by reception from such a creature. It led to peculiar vagaries. For example, the woman put her twin tentacles about the man and clung to him with no effort to rend or tear.

The idea of two creatures of the same species pleasurably anticipating being together without devouring each other – except during the Peace Tides, of course – is almost inconceivable to a Shadi. However, it appeared to be part of their normal psychology.

But this report grows long. I flowed upward and upward. The creatures in the Object experienced emotions which were stronger and ever stronger, and more and more remarkable. Successively the man reported to the woman that they were but four thousand of their 'feet' below the Surface, then two thousand, and then one. I was now completely possessed by curiosity. I had barely performed what turned out to be the last needed Morpt exercise and was moving still higher when my spatial sense suddenly gave me a new and incredible message. Above me, there was a barrier to its operation.

I cannot convey the feeling of finding a barrier to one's spatial sense. I was aware of my surroundings in every direction, but at a certain point above me there was suddenly – nothing! Nothing! At first it was alarming. I flowed up half my length, and the barrier grew nearer. Cautiously – even timorously – I flowed slowly nearer and nearer.

'Five hundred feet,' said the man inside the Object. 'My heavens, only five hundred feet! We should see glimmers of light through the ports. No, it's night now.'

I paused, debating. I was close enough to this barrier to reach up my first tentacle and touch it. I hesitated a long time. Then I did touch it. Nothing happened. I thrust my tentacle boldly through it. It went into Nothingness. Where it was there was no water. With an enormous emotion, I realized that above me was the central bubble and that I alone of living Shadi had reached and dared to touch it. The sensation in my tentacle within the bubble, above the Surface, was that of an enormous weight, as if the gas of departed Shadi would have thrust me back. But they did not attack, they did not even attempt to injure me.

Yes, I was splendidly proud. I felt like one who has overcome and consumed a Shadi of greater size than himself. And as I exulted, I became aware of the emotions of the creatures within the Object.

'Three hundred feet!' said the man frantically. 'It can't stop here! It can't! My dear, fate could not be so cruel!'

I found pleasure in the emotions of the two creatures. They felt a new emotion, now, which was as strange as any of my other experiences with them. It was an emotion which was the anticipation of other emotions. The woman named it.

'It is insane,' she told the man, 'but somehow I feel hope again.'

And in my pleasure and intellectual interest it seemed a very small thing for one who had already dared so greatly to continue the pleasures I felt. I flowed further up the slope. The barrier to my spatial sense – the Surface – came closer and ever closer.

'A hundred feet,' said the man in an emotion which to him was agony, but because of its novelty was a source of intellectual pleasure to me.

I transferred the Object to a forward tentacle and thrust it ahead. It bumped upon the solidity which here approached and actually penetrated the Surface. The man experienced a passion of the strong emotion called 'hope'.

'Twenty-five feet!' he cried. 'Darling, if we start to go down again, I'll open the hatch, and we'll go out as the bathysphere floods. I don't know whether we're near shore or not, but we'll try.'

The woman was pressed close against him. The agony of hope which filled her was a sensation which mingled with the high elation I felt over my own daring and achievement. I thrust the Object forward yet again. Here the Surface was so near the solidity under it that a part of my tentacle went above the Surface. And the emotions within the Object reached a climax. I thrust on, powerfully, against the weight within the Bubble, until the Object broke the surface, and then on and on until it was no longer in water but in gas, resting upon solidity which was itself touched only by gas.

The man and woman worked frantically within the Object. A part of it detached itself. They climbed out of it. They opened their maws and uttered cries. They wrapped their tentacles about each other and touched their maws together, not to devour but to express their emotions. They looked about them dazed with relief, and I saw through their eyes. The Surface stretched away for as far as their senses reported, moving and uneven, and yet flat. They stood upon solidity from which things projected upward. Overhead was a vast blackness, penetrated by innumerable small bright sources of light.

'Thank God!' said the man. 'To see trees and the stars again.'

They felt absolutely secure and at peace, as if in a Peace Tides enhanced a thousand fold. And perhaps I was intoxicated by my own daring or perhaps by the emotions I received from them. I thrust my tentacles through the Surface. Their weight was enormous, but my strength is great also.

Daringly I heaved up my body. I thrust my entire forepart through the Surface and into the central bubble. I was in the central bubble while still alive! My weight increased beyond computation, but for a long, proud interval I loomed above the Surface I saw with my own eyes – all eighty of them – the Surface beneath me and the patch of solidity on which the man and the woman stood. I, Sard, did this!

As I dipped below the Surface again I received the astounded thoughts of the creatures.

'A sea-serpent,' thought the man, and doubted his own sanity as I fear mine will be doubted. 'That's what did it.'

'Why not, darling?' the woman said calmly. 'It was a miracle, but people who love each other as we do simply couldn't be allowed to die.'

But the man stared at the Surface where I had vanished. I had caught his troubled thought.

'No one would believe it. They'd say we're insane. But confound it, here's the bathysphere, and our cable did break when we were above the Deep. When we're found, we'll simply say we don't know what happened and let them try to figure it out.'

I lay resting, close to the Surface, thinking many things. After a long time there was light. Fierce, unbearable light. It grew stronger and yet stronger. It was unbearable. It flowed down into the nearer depths.

That was many tides ago, because I dared not return to Honda with so vast a proportion of the gas in my swim-bladder released to the central bubble. I remained not too far below the Surface until my swim-bladder felt normal. I descended again and again waited until my 'immortal part' had replenished itself. It is difficult to feed upon such small creatures as inhabit the Heights. It took a long time for me to make the descent which by Morpt's discovery had been made so readily as an ascent. All my waking time was spent in the capture of food, and I had little time for meditation. I was never once full-fed in all the periods I paused to wait for my swim-bladder to be replenished. But when I returned to my cave, it had been occupied in my absence by another Shadi. I fed well.

Then came the Peace Tides. And now, having bred, I lay my report of my journey to the Surface at the service of all the Shadi. If I am decreed insane, I shall say no more. But this is my report. Now determine, O Shadi: Am I mad?

I, Morpt, in Peace Tides, have heard the report of Sard and having consulted with others of the Shadi, do declare that he has plainly confounded the imagined with the real.

His description of the scientific aspects of his journey, and which are not connected with the assumed creatures in the Object, are consistent with science. But it is manifestly impossible that any creature could live with its fellows permanently without the instinct to feed. It is manifestly impossible that creatures could live in gas. Distinction between light and light is patent nonsense. The psychology of such creatures as described by Sard is of the stuff of dreams.

Therefore, it is the consensus that Sard's report is not science. He may not be insane, however. The physiological effects of his admitted journey to great Heights have probably caused disorders in his body which have shown themselves in illusions. The scientific lessons to be learned from this report is that journeys to the Heights, though possible because of the exercises invented by myself, are extremely unwise and should never be made by Shadi. Given during the Peace Tides. . . .

PIPELINE TO PLUTO

Mood. Asimov makes the point that because of the particular disciplines of SF a good science-fiction writer can produce competent work in* any *field. Leinster was one of the rare exceptions that made the transition the other way. One of the advantages of this was that he was able to bring to his stories a sense of atmosphere that should be – but often is not – inseparable from most SF. Certainly the following item is a very chilly story in every respect.*

FAR, far out on Pluto, where the sun is only a very bright star and a frozen, airless globe circles in emptiness; far out on Pluto, there was motion. The perpetual faint starlight was abruptly broken. Yellow lights shone suddenly in a circle, and men in spacesuits waddled to a space tug – absurdly marked *Betsy-Anne* in huge white letters. They climbed up its side and went in the airlock. Presently a faint, jetting glow appeared below its drivetubes. It flared suddenly and the tug lifted, to hover expertly a brief distance above what seemed an unmarred field of frozen atmosphere. But that field heaved and broke. The nose of a Pipeline carrier appeared in the center of a cruciform opening. It thrust through. It stood half its length above the surface of the dead and lifeless planet. The tug drifted above it. Its grapnel dropped down, jetted minute flames, and engaged in the monster towring at the carrier's bow.

The tug's drivetubes flared luridly. The carrier heaved abruptly up out of its hidingplace and plunged for the heavens behind the tug. It had a huge classmark and number painted on its side, which was barely visible as it whisked out of sight. It

* 'So why aren't we rich?' *Nebula Award Stories* 8, Victor Gollancz, 1973.

went on up at four gravities acceleration, while the spacetug lined out on the most precise of courses and drove fiercely for emptiness.

A long, long time later, when Pluto was barely a pallid disk behind, the tug cast off. The carrier went on, sunward. Its ringed nose pointed unwaveringly to the sun toward which it would drift for years. It was one of a long, long line of carriers drifting through space, a day apart in time but millions of miles apart in distance. They would go on until a tug from Earth came out and grappled them and towed them in to their actual home planet.

But the *Betsy-Anne*, of Pluto, did not pause for contemplation of the two-billion-mile-long line of orecarriers taking the metal of pluto back to Earth. It darted off from the line its late tow now followed. Its radio-locator beam flickered invisibly in emptiness. Presently its course changed. It turned about. It braked violently, going up to six gravities deceleration for as long as half a minute at a time. Presently it came to rest and there floated toward it an object from Earth, a carrier with great white numerals on its sides. It had been hauled off Earth and flung into an orbit which would fetch it out to Pluto. The *Betsy-Anne*'s grapnel floated toward it and jetted tiny sparks until the towring was engaged. Then the tug and its new tow from Earth started back to Pluto.

There were two long lines of white-numbered carriers floating sedately through space. One line drifted tranquilly in to Earth. One drifted no less tranquilly out past the orbits of six planets to reach the closed-in, underground colony of the mines on Pluto.

Together they made up the Pipeline.

The evening Moon-rocket took off over to the north and went straight up to the zenith. Its blue-white rocket-flare changed color as it fell behind, until the tail-end was a deep, rich crimson. The Pipeline docks were silent, now, but opposite the yard the row of flimsy eating- and drinking-places rattled and thuttered to themselves from the lower-than-sound vibrations of the Moon-ship.

There was a youngish, battered man named Hill in the Pluto Bar, opposite the docks. He paid no attention to the Moon-rocket, but he looked up sharply as a man came out of the Pipeline gate and came across the street toward the bar. But Hill was staring at his drink when the door opened and the man from the dock looked the small dive over. Besides Hill – who looked definitely tough, and as if he had but recently recovered from a ravaging illness – there was only the bartender, a cata-wheel-truck driver and his girl having a drink together, and another man at a table by himself and fidgeting nervously as if he were waiting for someone. Hill's eyes flickered again to the man in the door. He looked suspicious. But then he looked back at his glass.

The other man came in and went to the bar.

'Evenin', Mr. Crowder,' said the bartender.

Hill's eyes darted up, and down again. The bartender reached below the bar, filled a glass, and slid it across the mahogany.

'Evenin',' said Crowder curtly. He looked deliberately at the fidgety man. He seemed to note that the fidgety man was alone. He gave no sign of recognition, but his features pinched a little, as some men's do when they feel a little, crawling unease. But there was nothing wrong except that the fidgety man seemed to be upset because he was waiting for someone who hadn't come.

Crowder sat down in a booth, alone. Hill waited a moment, looked sharply about him, and then stood up. He crossed purposefully to the booth in which Crowder sat.

'I'm lookin' for a fella named Crowder,' he said huskily. 'That's you, ain't it?'

Crowder looked at him, his face instantly masklike. Hill's looks matched his voice. There was a scar under one eye. He had a cauliflower ear. He looked battered, and hard-boiled – and as if he had just recovered from some serious injury or illness. His skin was reddened in odd patches.

'My name is Crowder,' said Crowder suspiciously. 'What is it?'

Hill sat down opposite him.

'My name's Hill,' he said in the same husky voice. 'There

was a guy who was gonna come here tonight. He'd fixed it up to be stowed away on a Pipeline carrier to Pluto. I bought 'im off. I bought his chance. I came here to take his place.'

'I don't know what you're talking about,' said Crowder coldly.

But he did. Hill could see that he did. His stomach-muscles knotted. He was uneasy. Hill's gaze grew scornful.

'You're the night super of th' Pipeline yards, ain't you?' he demanded truculently.

Crowder's face stayed masklike. Hill looked tough. He looked like the sort of yegg who'd get into trouble with the police because he'd never think things out ahead. He knew it, and he didn't care. Because he had gotten in trouble – often – because he didn't think things out ahead. But he wasn't that way tonight. He'd planned tonight in detail.

'Sure I'm the night superintendent of the Pipeline yards,' said Crowder shortly. 'I came over for a drink. I'm going back. But I don't know what you're talking about.'

Hill's eyes grew hard.

'Listen, fella,' he said truculently – but he had been really ill, and the signs of it were plain – 'they're payin' five hundred credits a day in the mines out on Pluto, ain't they? A guy works a year out there, he comes back rich, don't he?'

'Sure!' said Crowder. 'The wages got set by law when it cost a lot to ship supplies out. Before the Pipeline got going.'

'An' they ain't got enough guys to work, have they?'

'There's a shortage,' agreed Crowder coldly. 'Everybody knows it. The liners get fifty thousand credits for a one-way passage, and it takes six months for the trip.'

Hill nodded, truculently.

'I wanna get out to Pluto,' he said huskily. 'See? They don't ask too many questions about a guy when he turns up out there. But the space liners, they do, an' they want too many credits. So I wanna go out in a carrier by Pipeline. See?'

Hill downed his drink and stood up.

'There's a law,' he said uncompromisingly, 'that says the Pipeline can't carry passengers or mail. The spacelines jammed that through. Politics.'

'Maybe,' said Hill pugnaciously, 'but you promised to let a guy stow away on the carrier tonight. He told me about it. I paid him off. He sold me his place. I'm takin' it, see?'

'I'm night superintendent at the yards,' Crowder told him. 'If there are arrangements for stowaways, I don't know about them. You're talking to the wrong man.'

He abruptly left the table. He walked across the room to the fidgety man, who seemed more and more uneasy because somebody hadn't turned up. Crowder's eyes were viciously angry when he bent over the fidgety man.

'Look here, Moore!' he said savagely, in a low tone. 'That guy is on! He says he paid your passenger to let him take his place. That's why your man hasn't showed up. You picked him out and he sold his place to this guy. So I'm leaving it right in your lap! I can lie myself clear. They couldn't get any evidence back, anyhow. Not for years yet. But what he told me is straight, he's got to go or he'll shoot off his mouth! So it's in your lap!'

The eyes of Moore – the fidgety man – had a hunted look in them. He swallowed as if his mouth were dry. But he nodded.

Crowder went out. Hill scowled after him. After a moment he came over to Moore.

'Lookahere,' he said huskily. 'I wanna know somethin'. That guy's night super for Pipeline, ain't he?'

Moore nodded. He licked his lips.

'Lissen!' said Hill angrily, 'there's a Pipeline carrier leaves here every day for Pluto, an' one comes in from Pluto every day. It's just like gettin' on a 'copter an' goin' from one town to another on the Pipeline, ain't it?'

Moore nodded again – this time almost unnoticeably.

'That's what a guy told me,' said Hill pugnaciously. 'He said he'd got it all fixed up to stow away on a carrier-load of grub. He said he'd paid fifteen hundred credits to have it fixed up. He was gonna leave tonight. I paid him off to let me take his place. Now this guy Crowder tells me I'm crazy!'

'I . . . wouldn't know anything about it,' said Moore, hesitantly. 'I know Crowder, but that's all.'

Hill growled to himself. He doubled up his fist and looked at it. It was a capable fist. There were scars on it as proof that things had been hit with it.

'O.K.!' said Hill. 'I guess that guy kidded me. He done me outta plenty credits. I know where to find him. He's goin' to a hospital!'

He stirred, scowling.

'W-wait a minute,' said Moore. 'It seems to me I heard something, once—'

Carriers drifted on through space. They were motorless, save for the tiny drives for the gyros in their noses. They were a hundred feet long, and twenty feet thick, and some of them contained foodstuffs in air-sealed containers – because everything will freeze, in space, but even ice will evaporate in a vacuum. Some carried drums of rocket fuel for the tugs and heaters and the generators for the mines on Pluto. Some contained tools and books and visiphone records and caviar and explosives and glue and cosmetics for the women on Pluto. But all of them drifted slowly, leisurely, unhurriedly, upon their two-billion-mile journey.

They were the Pipeline. You put a carrier into the line at Earth, headed out to Pluto. The same day you took a carrier out of space at the end of the line, at Pluto. You put one into the Earth-bound line, on Pluto. You took one out of space the same day, on Earth. There was continuous traffic between the two planets, with daily arrivals and departures from each. But passenger-traffic between Earth and Pluto went by space liners, at a fare of fifty thousand credits for the trip. Because even the liners took six months for the journey, and the Pipeline carriers – well, there were over twelve hundred of them in each line going each way, a day apart in time and millions of miles apart in space. They were very lonely, those long cylinders with their white-painted numbers on their sides. The stars were the only eyes to look upon the while they traveled, and it took three years to drift from one end of the pipeline to the other.

But nevertheless there were daily arrivals and departures on the Pipeline, and there was continuous traffic between the two planets.

Moore turned away from the pay-visiphone, into which he had talked in a confidential murmur while the screen remained blank. The pugnacious, battered Hill scowled impatiently behind him.

'I'm not sure,' said Moore uneasily. 'I talked to somebody I thought might know something, but they're cagey. They'd lose their jobs and maybe get in worse trouble if anybody finds out they're smuggling stowaways to Pluto. Y'see, the space lines have a big pull in politics. They've got it fixed so the Pipeline can't haul anything but freight. If people could travel by Pipeline, the space liners 'ud go broke. So they watch close.'

He looked uneasy as he spoke. His eyes watched Hill almost alarmedly. But Hill said sourly:

'O.K.! I'm gonna find the guy that sold me his place, an' I'm gonna write a message on him with a blowtorch. The docs'll have fun readin' him, an' why he's in the hospital!'

Moore swallowed.

'Who was it? I've heard something—'

Hill bit off the name. Moore swallowed again – as if the name meant something. As if it were right.

'I . . . I'll tell you, guy,' said Moore. 'It's none of my business, but I . . . well . . . I might be able to fix things up for you. It's risky, though, butting in on something that ain't my business—'

'How much?' said Hill shortly.

'Oh . . . f-five hundred,' said Moore uneasily.

Hill stared at him. Hard. Then he pulled a roll out of his pocket. He displayed it.

'I got credits,' he said huskily. 'But I'm givin' you just one hundred of 'em. I'll give you nine hundred more when I'm all set. That's twice what you asked for. But that's all, see? I got a reason to get off Earth, an' tonight, I'll pay to manage it. But if I'm double-crossed, somebody gets hurt!'

Moore grinned nervously.

'No double-crossing in this,' he said quickly. 'Just . . . well . . . it is ticklish.'

'Yeah,' said Hill. He waved a battered-knuckled hand. 'Get goin'. Tell those guys I'm willin' to pay. But I get stowed away, or I'll fix that guy who sold me his place so he'll tell all he knows! I'm goin' to Pluto, or else!'

Moore said cautiously:

'M-maybe you'll have to pay out a little more . . . but not much! But you'll get there! I've heard . . . just heard, you understand . . . that the gang here smuggles a fella into the Pipeline yard and up into the nose of a carrier loaded with grub. Champagne and all that. He can live high on the way, and not worry because out on Pluto they're so anxious to get a man to work that they'll square things. They need men bad, out on Pluto! They pay five hundred credits a day!'

'Yeah,' said Hill grimly. 'They need 'em so bad there ain't no extradition either. I'm int'rested in that, too. Now get goin' an' fix me up!'

The Pipeline was actually a two-billion-mile arrangement of specks in infinity. Each of the specks was a carrier. Each of the carriers was motorless and inert. Each was unlighted. Each was lifeless. But – some of them had contained life when they started.

The last carrier out from Earth, to be sure, contained nothing but its proper cargo of novelties, rocket fuel, canned goods and plastic base. But in the one beyond that, there was what had been a hopeful stowaway. A man, with his possessions neatly piled about him. He'd been placed up in the nose of the carrier, and he'd waited, mousy-still, until the space tug connected with the tow ring and heaved the carrier out to the beginning of the Pipeline. As a stowaway, he hadn't wanted to be discovered. The carrier ahead of that – many millions of miles farther out – contained two girls, who had heard that stenographers were highly paid on Pluto, and that there were so few women that a girl might take her pick of husbands. The one just before that had a man and woman in it. There were four men in the carrier beyond them.

The hundred-foot cylinders drifting out and out and out toward Pluto contained many stowaways. The newest of them still looked quite human. They looked quite tranquil. After all, when a carrier is hauled aloft at four gravities acceleration the air flows out of the bilge-valves very quickly, but the cold comes in more quickly still. None of the stowaways had actually suffocated. They'd frozen so suddenly they probably did not realize what was happening. At sixty thousand feet the temperature is around seventy degrees below zero. At a hundred and twenty thousand feet it's so cold that figures simply haven't any meaning. And at four gravities acceleration you reach a hundred and twenty thousand feet before you've really grasped the fact that you paid all your money to be flung unprotected into space. So you never quite realize that you're going on out into a vacuum which will gradually draw every atom of moisture from every tissue of your body.

But, though there were many stowaways, not one had yet reached Pluto. They would do so in time, of course. But the practice of smuggling stowaways to Pluto had only been in operation for a year and a half. The first of the deluded ones had not quite passed the halfway mark. So the stowaway business should be safe and profitable for at least a year and a half more. Then it would be true that a passenger entered the Pipeline from Earth and a passenger reached Pluto on the same day. But it would not be the same passenger, and there would be other differences. Even then, though, the racket would simply stop being profitable, because there was no extradition either to or from Pluto.

So the carriers drifting out through emptiness with their stowaways were rather ironic, in a way. There were tragedies within them, and nothing could be done about them. It was ironic that the carriers gave no sign of the freight they bore. They moved quite sedately, quite placidly, with a vast leisure among the stars.

The battered youngish man said coldly: 'Well? You fixed it?'

Moore grinned nervously.

'Yeah. It's all fixed. At first they thought you might be an undercover man for the passenger lines, trying to catch the Pipeline smuggling passengers so they could get its charter canceled. But they called up the man whose place you took, and it's straight. He said he gave you his place and told you to see Crowder.'

Hill said angrily:

'But he stalled me!'

Moore licked his lips.

'You'll get the picture in a minute. We cross the street and go in the Pipeline yard. You have to slip the guard something. A hundred credits for looking the other way.'

Hill growled:

'No more stalling!'

'No more stalling,' promised Moore. 'You go out to Pluto in the next carrier.'

They went out of the Pluto Bar. They crossed the street, which was thin, black, churned-up mud from the catawheel trucks which hauled away each day's arrival of freight from Pluto. They moved directly and openly for the gateway. The guard strolled toward them.

'Slim,' said Moore, grinning nervously, 'meet my friend Hill.'

'Sure!' said the guard.

He extended his hand, palm up. Hill put a hundred-credit note in it.

'O.K.,' said the guard. 'Luck on Pluto, fella.'

He turned his back. Moore snickered almost hysterically and led the way into the dark recesses of the yard. There was the landing field for the space tugs. There were six empty carriers off to one side. There was one in a loading pit, sunk down on a hydraulic platform until only its nose now showed aboveground. It could be loaded in its accelerating position, that way, and would not need to be upended after reaching maximum weight.

'Take-off is half an hour before sunrise today,' said Moore jerkily. 'You'll know when it's coming because the hydraulic platform shoves the carrier up out of the pit. Then you'll hear the grapnel catching in the towring. Then you start. The tug puts you in the Pipeline and hangs around and picks up the other carrier coming back.'

'That's speed!' said Hill. 'Them scientists are great stuff, huh? I start off in that, an' before I know it I'm on Pluto'!

'Yeah,' said Moore. He smirked with a twitching, ghastly effect. 'Before you know it. Here's the door where you go in.'

Crowder came around the other side of the carrier's cone-shaped nose. He scowled at Hill, and Hill scowled back.

'You sounded phony to me,' said Crowder ungraciously. 'I wasn't going to take any chances by admitting anything. Moore told you it's going to cost you extra?'

'For what?' demanded Hill, bristling.

'Because you've got to get away fast,' said Crowder evenly. 'Because there's no extradition from Pluto. We're not in this for our health. Two thousand credits more.'

Hill snarled:

'Thief—' Then he said sullenly. 'O.K.'

'And my nine hundred,' said Moore eagerly.

'Sure,' said Hill, sardonically. He paid. 'O.K. now? Whadda I do now?'

'Go in the door here,' said Crowder. 'The cargo's grub. Get comfortable and lay flat on your back when you feel the carrier coming up to be hitched on for towing. After the acceleration's over and you're in the Pipeline, do as you please.'

'Yeah!' said Moore, giggling nervously. 'Do just as you please.'

Hill said tonelessly:

'Right. I'll start now.'

He moved with a savage, infuriated swiftness. There was a queer, muffled cracking sound. Then a startled gasp from Moore, a moment's struggle, and another sharp crack.

Hill went into the nose of the carrier. He dragged them in. He stayed inside for minutes. He came out and listened, swinging a leather blackjack meditatively. Then he went over to the gate. He called cautiously to the guard.

'You! Slim! Crowder says come quick – an' quiet! Somethin's happened an' him an' Moore got their hands full.'

The guard blinked, and then came quickly. Hill hurried behind him to the loading pit. As the guard called tensely:

'Hey, Crowder, what's the matter—'

Hill swung the blackjack again, with a certain deft precision. The guard collapsed.

A little later Hill had finished his work. The three men were bound with infinite science. They not only could not escape, they could not even kick. That's quite a trick – but it can be done if you study the art. And they were not only gagged, but there was tape over their mouths beyond the gag, so that they could not even make a respectable groaning noise. And Hill surveyed the three of them by the light of a candle he had taken from his pocket – as he had taken the rope from about his waist – and said in husky satisfaction:

'O.K. O.K.! I'm givin' you fellas some bad news. You're headin' out to Pluto.'

Terror close to madness shone in the three pairs of eyes which fixed frantically upon him. The eyes seemed to threaten to start from their sockets.

'It ain't so bad,' said Hill grimly. 'Not like you think it is. You'll get there before you know it. No kidding! You'll go snakin' up at four gravities, an' the air'll go out. But you won't die of that. Before you strangle, you'll freeze – an' fast! You'll freeze so fast y'won't have time to die, fellas. That's the funny part. You freeze so quick you ain't got time to die! The Space Patrol found out a year or so back that that can happen, when things are just right – an' they will be, for you. So the Space Patrol will be all set to bring you back, when y' get to Pluto. But it does hurt, fellas. It hurts like hell! I oughta know!'

He grinned at them, his mouth twisted and his eyes grim.

'I paid you fellas to send me out to Pluto last year. But it happened I didn't get to Pluto. The Patrol dragged my carrier out o' the Pipeline an' over to Callisto because they hadda shortage o' rocket fuel there. So I' been through it, an' it hurts! I wouldn't tell on you fellas, because I wanted you to have it, so I took my bawlin' out for stowin' away an' come back to send you along. So you' goin', fellas! An' you' goin' all the way to

Pluto! And remember this, fellas! It's gonna be good! After they bring you back, out there on Pluto, every fella an' every soul you sent off as stowaways, they'll be there on Pluto waitin' for you. It's gonna be good, guys! It's gonna be good!'

He looked at them in the candlelight, and seemed to take a vast satisfaction in their expressions. Then he blew out the candle, and closed the nose door of the carrier, and went away.

And half an hour before sunrise next morning the hydraulic platform pushed the carrier up, and a space tug hung expertly overhead and its grapnel came down and hooked in the tow-ring, and then the carrier jerked skyward at four gravities acceleration.

Far out from Earth, the carrier went on, the latest of a long line of specks in infinity which constituted the Pipeline to Pluto. Many of those specks contained things which had been human – and would be human again. But now each one drifted sedately away from the sun, and in the later carriers the stowaways still looked completely human and utterly tranquil. What had happened to them had come so quickly that they did not realize what it was. But in the last carrier of all, with three bound, gagged figures in its nose, the expressions were not tranquil at all. Because those men did know what had happened to them. More – they knew what was yet to come.

SAM, THIS IS YOU

Romance. Because of his association with the general-fiction market Leinster was more at home in this area than were most of his contemporaries. Doc 'Lensman' Smith, who had to have his love scenes written for him, was at least being honest in his recognition that SF & romance can be an oil-and-water mix. Even Leinster preferred to avoid problems by spicing his love-interest with humor, as in his familiar 'Fourth Dimensional Demonstrator'. However, the following lesser-known story is very definitely a more craftsman-like piece of work.

YOU are not supposed to believe this story, and, if you ask Sam Yoder about it, he is apt to say that it's all a lie. But Sam is a bit sensitive about it. He doesn't want the question of privacy to be raised again – especially in Rosie's hearing. And there are other matters. But it's all perfectly respectable and straightforward. It could have happened to anybody – well, almost anybody. Anybody, say, who was a telephone lineman for the Batesville and Rappahannock Telephone Company, who happened to be engaged to Rosie and who had been told admiringly by Rosie that anybody as smart as he was ought to do something wonderful and get rich – and, of course, anybody who'd taken that seriously, had been puttering around on a device to make private conversations on a party-line telephone possible and almost had the trick.

It began about six o'clock on July second, when Sam was up a telephone pole near Bridge's Run. He was hunting for the place where that party line had gone dead. He'd hooked in his lineman's phone, and, since he couldn't raise Central, he was just going to start looking for the break when his phone rang back. The line had checked dead both ways from this spot, but when the call-bell rang he put the receiver to his ear.

'Hello,' said Sam. 'Who's this?'

'Sam,' said a voice, 'this is you.'

'Huh?' said Sam. 'What's that?'

'This is you,' the voice on the wire repeated. 'You, Sam Yoder. Don't you recognize your own voice? This is you, Sam Yoder, calling from the twelfth of July. Don't hang up!'

Sam didn't even think of hanging up. He was pained. He was up a telephone pole trying to do some work, resting in his safety belt and with his climbing-irons safely fixed in the wood. Naturally, he thought somebody was trying to joke with him, and when a man is working is no time for practical jokes.

'I'm not hanging up,' Sam said dourly, 'but you'd better!'

The voice was familiar, but he couldn't quite place it. If it talked a little more, he knew he would. He knew it just about as well as he knew his own, and it was irritating not to be able to call this joker by name.

The voice said, 'Sam, it's the second of July where you are, and you're up a pole by Bridge's Run. The line's dead in two places, else I couldn't talk to you. Lucky, ain't it?'

Sam said formidably, 'Whoever you are, it ain't going to be lucky for you if you ever need telephone service and you've kept wasting my time. I'm busy!'

'But I'm you!' the voice insisted persuasively. 'And you're me! We're both the same Sam Yoder, only where I am it's July twelfth. Where you are it's July second. You've heard of time-traveling, but that's nonsense. That won't work. But this is time-talking, and it does work! You're talking to yourself – that's me – and I'm talking to myself – that's you – and it looks like we've got a mighty good chance to get rich.'

Then something came into Sam's memory, and he stiffened. Every muscle in his body went taut and tight, even as he was saying to himself, 'It can't be!' But he'd remembered hearing somewhere that, if a man goes and stands in a corner and talks to the wall, his voice will sound to him just like it sounds to somebody else. And being in the telephone business he'd tried it. And now he did recognize the voice. It was his. His own.

Talking to him. Which, of course, was impossible, only it appeared to be a fact.

'Look,' Sam said hoarsely, 'I don't believe this!'

'Then listen,' said the voice briskly. And it was his own voice. There couldn't be any more mistake about it than if he'd been looking in a mirror at his own face. But in about half a minute Sam's face began to get red. It burned. His ears began to feel scorched. Because the voice – his voice – was telling him strictly private anecdotes that nobody else in the world knew. Nobody but he and Rosie.

'Quit it!' Sam groaned. 'Either you or me is crazy! Or you're Old Scratch! Quit it! Somebody might be listening. Tell me what you want and ring off!'

The voice – his own voice – told him what it wanted. It sounded pleased. It told him precisely what it wanted him to do. And then, very kindly, it told him exactly where the two breaks in the line were. And then it rang off.

Sam sweated when he looked at the first of the two places. The break was there, all right. He fixed it. He looked at the second place, where a joining was bad, and he fixed that. It was where his voice had said it would be. And that was as impossible as anything else. When he'd fixed the second dead place Sam called Central and told her he was sick and was going home and that, if there were any other phones that needed fixing today, people were probably better off without phone service, anyhow.

He went home, washed his face, and made himself a brew of coffee and drank it – but none of his memory changed. Presently he heard himself muttering.

So he said defiantly, 'There ain't any crazy people in my family, so it ain't likely I've gone out of my head. But Gawd knows nobody but Rosie knows about me telling her sentimental that her nose is so cute I couldn't believe she'd ever had to blow it! Maybe it was me, talking to myself.'

Talking to oneself is not abnormal. Lots of people do it. But Sam missed the implication he could have drawn from the fact that he'd answered himself back. He reasoned painfully.

'If somebody drove over to Rappahannock, past Dunnsville,

and telephoned back that there was a brush fire at Dunnsville, I wouldn't be surprised to get to Dunnsville and find a brush fire there. So, if somebody phones back from next Tuesday that Mr. Broaddus broke his leg next Tuesday – why, I shouldn't be surprised to get to next Tuesday and find he done it. Going to Rappahannock past Dunnsville and going to next Thursday past next Tuesday ain't so much difference. It's only the difference between a road-map and a calendar!'

Then he began to see implications. He blinked.

'Yes, sir!' he said, in awe. 'I wouldn't've thought of it if I hadn't told myself on the telephone, but there is money to be made out of this! I must be near as smart as Rosie thinks I am! I'd better get that dinkus set up!'

He set to work in some enthusiasm. He'd more or less half-heartedly worked out an idea of how a party-line telephone conversation could be made private, and just out of instinct he'd accumulated a lot of stuff around the house that should have been on the phone company's inventory. There were condensers and phone-microphones and selective-ringing bells and resistances and the like. He'd meant to put some of them together some day and see what happened. But he'd been too busy courting Rosie to get at it.

Now he did get to work. His own voice on the telephone had told him to. It'd warned him that one thing he'd intended wouldn't work, but something else would. It was essentially simple, after all. He finished it, cut off his line from Central and hooked the gadget in. He rang. Half a minute later somebody rang back.

'Hello!' said Sam, sweating. He'd broken the line to Central, remember. In theory, he shouldn't have gotten anybody anywhere.

But a very familiar voice said, 'Hello,' back at him, and Sam swallowed and said, 'Hello, Sam! This is you in the second of July.'

The voice at the other end agreed cordially. It said that Sam had done pretty well, and now the two of them – Sam in the here and now and Sam in the middle of the week after next – would proceed to get rich together. But the voice from July twelfth seemed less absorbed in the conversation than Sam thought quite right. It seemed even abstracted. And Sam was at once sweating from the pure unreasonableness of the affair and conscious that he rated congratulations for the highly technical device he had built. After all, not everybody could build a time-talker! He said with some irony, 'If you're too busy to talk—'

'I'll tell you,' said the voice from the twelfth of July, gratified. 'I am kind of busy right now. You'll understand when you get to where I am. Don't get mad, Sam! Tell you what! You go see Rosie, and tell her about this and have a nice evening together. Ha ha!'

'Now what,' Sam said cagily, 'do you mean by that "Ha ha"?'

'You'll find out,' said the voice. 'Knowin' what I know, I'll even double it. Ha ha, ha ha!'

There was a click. Sam yapped at the dead telephone. He rang back, but got no answer. He may have been the first man in history to take an instinctive and completely sincere dislike to himself for good cause. But presently he muttered, 'Smart, huh? There's two can play at that. I'm the one that's got to do things if we are both goin' to get rich.'

He put his gadget away carefully, parted his hair, ate some cold food around the house and drove over to see Rosie. It was a night and an errand that ordinarily would have seemed purely romantic. There were fireflies floating about, and the moon shone down splendidly, and a perfumed breeze carried mosquitos from one place to another. It was the sort of night on which ordinarily Sam would have thought only of Rosie, and Rosie would have optimistic ideas about how housekeeping could, after all, be conducted on what Sam made a week.

They got settled down in the hammock on Rosie's front porch, and Sam said expansively, 'Rosie, I've made up my mind to get rich. You ought to have everything your little heart desires. Suppose you tell me what you want so I'll know how rich I've got to get?'

Rosie drew back. She looked sharply at Sam.

'Do you feel all right, Sam?'

He beamed at her. He'd never been married, and he didn't

know how crazy it sounded to Rosie to be queried on how much money would satisfy her. There simply isn't any answer to that question.

'Listen,' Sam said tenderly. 'Nobody knows it, but tonight Joe Hunt and the Widow Backus are eloping romantic to North Carolina to get married. We'll find out about it tomorrow. And day after tomorrow, on the folrth of July, Dunnsville is going to win the baseball game with Bradensberg, seven to five, all tied till the ninth inning, and then George Peeby is going to hit a homer with Fred Holmes on second base.'

Rosie stared at him. Sam explained complacently. The Sam Yoder in the middle of the week after next had told him what to expect in those particular cases. He would tell him other things to expect, so Sam was going to get rich.

Rosie said, 'Sam! Somebody was playing a joke on you!'

'Yeah?' Sam said comfortably. 'Who else but me knows what you said to me that time you thought I was mad with you and you were crying out back of the well-house?'

'Sam!' said Rosie.

'And,' Sam went on, 'nobody else knows about that time we were picknicking and a bug got down the back of your dress and you thought it was a hornet.'

'Sam Yoder!' wailed Rosie. 'You never told anybody about that!'

'Nope,' Sam said truthfully, 'I never did. But the me in the week after next knew. He told me! So he had to be me talking to me. Couldn't've been anybody else.'

Rosie gasped. Sam explained all over again. In detail. When he had finished, Rosie seemed dazed.

Then she said desperately, 'S-sam! Either you've t-told somebody else everything we ever said or did together, or else – else there's somebody who knows every word we ever said to each other. That's awful! Do you really and truly mean to tell me—'

'Sure I mean to tell you,' Sam said happily. 'The me in the week after next called me up and talked about things nobody knows but you and me. Can't be no doubt at all!'

Rosie shivered. Then she chattered, 'He – he knows every word we ever said. Then he knows every word we're saying now!' She gulped. 'Sam Yoder, you go home!'

Sam gaped at her. She got up and backed away from him.

'D-do you think,' she said despairingly, 'that I – that I'm g-going to talk to you when – s-somebody else listens to every w-word I say and – knows everything I do? D-do you think I'm going to *m-marry* you, Sam Yoder?'

Then she ran away, weeping noisily, slammed the door on Sam and wouldn't come out again. Her father came out presently, looking patient, and asked Sam to go home so Rosie could finish crying and he could read his newspaper in peace.

On the way back to his own house Sam meditated darkly. By the time he got home he was furious. The him in the week after next could have warned him about this! When he got home he rang and rang and rang on the cutoff line, with his gadget hooked in to call July the Twelfth. But there was no answer.

When morning came he rang again, but there was still no answer. He loaded his tool-kit in the truck and went off to work feeling about as low as a man could feel.

He felt lower when he reported at the office and somebody told him excitedly that Joe Hunt and the Widow Backus had eloped to North Carolina to get married. Nobody'd have tried to stop them if they'd gotten married prosaically at home, but they'd eloped to make things more romantic.

It wasn't romantic to Sam. It was devastating proof that there was another him ten days off, knowing everything he knew and more besides, and very likely laughing his head off at the fix Sam was in. Because, obviously, Rosie would be still more convinced when she heard this news. She'd know Sam wasn't crazy or the victim of a practical joke. He'd told the truth.

It wasn't the first time a man got in trouble with a woman by telling her the truth, but it was new to Sam. It hurt.

He went over to Bradensburg that day to repair some broken lines, and around noon he went into a store to get something to eat. There were some local sportsmen in the store, bragging to each other about what the Bradensburg baseball team would do to the Dunnsville nine on the morrow.

Sam said peevishly, 'Huh! Dunnsville will win that game by two runs!'

A local sportsman said pugnaciously:

'Have you got any money that agrees with you? If you have, put it up and let somebody cover it!'

Sam wanted to draw back. But he had roused the civic pride of Bradensburg. He tried to temporize, and he was jeered at. In the end, indignantly, he dragged out all the money he had with him and bet it – eleven dollars. It was covered instantly, amid raucous laughter. And on the way back to Batesville he reflected unhappily that he was going to make eleven dollars out of knowing what was going to happen in the ninth inning of that ball game, but it looked like he'd lost Rosie.

He tried to call the other himself up again that night. There was no more answer than before. He unhooked the gadget and restored normal service to himself. He called Rosie's house. She answered the phone herself.

'Rosie,' Sam said yearningly, 'are you still mad with me?'

'I never was mad with you,' said Rosie, gulping. 'I'm mad with whoever was talking to you on that phone and knows all our private affairs. And I'm mad with you if you told him.'

'But I didn't tell him!' Sam said despairingly. 'He's me! All he has to do is just remember! I tried to call him again last night and again this morning,' he added bitterly, 'and he don't answer. Maybe he's gone off somewheres. I'm thinking it might be a – a kind of illusion, maybe.'

'You said there'd be an elopement last night,' said Rosie, her voice wabbling. 'And there was. Joe Hunt and the Widow Backus. Just like you said!'

'It – it could've been a coincidence,' said Sam, not too hopefully.

'I'm – w-waiting,' Rosie said shakily, 'to see if Dunnsville beats Bradensburg seven to five tomorrow, tied to the ninth, with George Peeby hitting a homer then with Fred Holmes on second base. If – if that happens, I'll – I'll die!'

'Why?' asked Sam.

'Because,' Rosie wailed, 'it'll mean that I can't m-marry you ever, because s-somebody else'd be looking over your shoulder and we wouldn't ever be by ourselves all our lives, night or day!'

She hung up, weeping, and Sam swore slowly and steadily and with venom. As he swore, he worked to hook up his device again. And then Sam rang, and rang, and rang. But he didn't answer.

Next day, in the big Fourth of July game, Dunnsville beat Bradensburg seven to five. It was tied to the ninth. Then George Peeby hit a homer with Fred Holmes on second base. Sam collected eleven dollars in winnings, but he could have wept.

He stayed home that night, brooding and every so often trying to call himself up on the device he had invented and been told – by himself – to modify. It was a nice gadget, but Sam did not enjoy it. It was a nice night, too. There was moonlight. But Sam did not enjoy that, either. Moonlight wouldn't do Sam any good as long as there was another him in the middle of the week after next, refusing to talk to him so he could get out of the fix he was in.

But next morning the phone-bell woke him up. He swore at it out of habit until he got out of bed, and then he realized that his gadget was hooked in and Central was cut off. Then he made it in one jump to the instrument.

'Hello!'

'Don't fret,' said his own voice, patronizingly. 'Rosie's going to make up with you.'

'How in blazes d'you know what she's going to do?' Sam raged. 'She won't marry me with you hanging around! I've been trying to figure out a way to get rid of you—'

'Hush up!' said the voice on the telephone, impatiently. 'I'm busy! I've got to go collect the money you've made for us.'

'You collect money?' roared Sam. 'I get in trouble and you collect money?'

'I have to collect it,' his voice said with the impatient patience of one speaking to a small and idiot child, 'before you can have it. Listen here! Where you are it's Tuesday. You're going over to Dunnsville today to fix some phones. You'll be in Mr. Broaddus's law office about half-past ten. You look out the window and notice a fella sitting in a car in front of the bank. Notice him good!'

'I won't do it,' Sam said defiantly. 'I ain't taking any orders from you! Maybe you're me, but I make money and you collect it. For all I know you spend it before I get to it! I'm quitting this business right now! It's cost me my own true love and all my life's happiness and to hell with you!'

His own voice sounded singularly sarcastic, in reply: 'You won't do it? Wait and see!'

So that morning the telephone company manager told Sam, when he reported for work, to drive over to Dunnsville and check on some lines there. Sam balked. He said there were much more important lines needing repair elsewhere. The company manager explained gently to Sam that Mr. Broaddus over in Dunnsville had been taken down drunk at a Fourth of July party and had fallen out of a window. He'd broken his leg. So it was a Christian duty to make sure he had a telephone in working order in his office, and Sam would get over there right away – or else.

On the way to Dunnsville, brooding, Sam remembered that he'd known about Mr. Broaddus's leg. He had told himself about it on the telephone. He ground his teeth. At half-past ten, he was fixing Mr. Broaddus's telephone when he remembered about the man he was supposed to get a good look at, sitting in a car in front of the bank. He made a bitter resolution not to glance outside of the lawyer's office under any circumstances. He meditated savagely that by this resolution the schemes of his other self in the future were abolished.

Naturally, he presently went to the window and looked to see what he was abolishing.

There was a car before the bank, with a reddish-haired man sitting in it. A haze came out of the exhaust-pipe, showing that the motor was running. None of this impressed Sam as remarkable. But, as he looked, two other men came running out of the bank. One of them was carrying a bag, and both of them had revolvers out and waving, and they piled into the car. The reddish-haired man gunned it, and it was abruptly a dwindling speck in a cloud of dust, getting out of town.

Three seconds later old Mr. Bluford, president of the bank, came out yelling, and the cashier came after him, and it was a first-rate bank robbery they were yelling about. The men in the getaway-car had departed with thirty-five thousand dollars in lawful money unlawfully acquired. And all of it had happened so fast that Sam hardly realized what *had* happened when he went interestedly out to see what it was all about. He was instantly seized upon to do some work. The bank robbers had shot out the telephone cable out of town with a shotgun, so word of their dastardly deed couldn't get ahead of them. Sam was needed to re-establish communications with the outside world.

He did that little thing, absorbedly reflecting on the details of the robbery as he'd heard them. He was high up on a telephone pole and the sheriff and enthusiastic citizens were streaking past in cars to make his labors unnecessary, when the personal aspect of all this affair hit him.

'Migawd!' said Sam, shocked. 'That me in the middle of next week told me to come over here and watch a bank robbery! But he didn't let on what was going to happen so's I could stop it!' He felt an incredulous indignation come over him. 'I woulda been a hero!' he said resentfully. 'Rosie woulda admired me! That other me is a born crook!'

Then he realized the facts. The other him was himself, only a week and a half distant. The other him was so far sunk in dastardliness that he permitted a crime to take place, with no more than sardonic amusement. And there was nothing he could do about it. He couldn't even tell the authorities about this depraved character! They wouldn't believe him unless he could get his other self on the telephone and make him admit his criminality, and then what could they do?

Sam felt what little zest had seemed to be left in living go trickling away. He looked into the future and saw nothing desirable in it. He finished the repair of the shot-out telephone line painstakingly; then he went down to his truck and drove over to Rosie's house. There wasn't but one thing he could do.

Rosie came to the door suspiciously.

'I come to tell you good-by, Rosie,' said Sam. 'I just found out I'm a criminal, so I aim to go and commit my crimes far away from my home and the friends who never thought I'd turn out this way. Good-by, Rosie!'

'You, Sam!' said Rosie. 'What's happened now?'

He told her. About the bank robbery and how his own self – in the week after next – had known it was going to happen, and told Sam to go watch it without giving him information by which it could have been stopped.

'He knew it after it happened,' said Sam bitterly, 'and he could've told me about it before! He didn't. So he's a accessory to the crime. And he is me, so that makes me a accessory, too. Good-by, Rosie, my own true love! You'll never see me more!'

'You set right down here,' Rosie commanded, firmly. 'You haven't done a thing yet! So it's that other you who's a criminal. You haven't got a thing to run away for.'

'But I'm going to have!' said Sam despairingly. 'I'm doomed to be a criminal! It's that me in the week after next! There's nothing to be done!'

'Says who?' Rosie said grimly. '*I'm* going to do something.'

'What?' asked Sam.

'I'm going to reform you,' said Rosie, 'before you start!'

She was a determined girl, that Rosie. She marched into the house and got into her blue jeans. She went to her father's woodshed, where he kept his tools, got a monkey wrench and put it in her hip pocket. When she came to the truck, Sam said:

'What's the idea, Rosie?'

'I'm riding around with you,' said Rosie, with a grim air. 'You won't do anything criminal with me on hand! And if that other you starts talking to you on the telephone I'm going to climb that pole and tell him where he gets off!'

'If anybody could keep me from turning criminal,' Sam acknowledged, 'it'd be you, Rosie. But that monkey wrench – what's it for?'

Rosie climbed into the seat beside him.

'You start having criminal ideas,' she told him, 'and you'll find out! Now you go on about your business and I and the monkey wrench will look after your morals!'

And things went on from there. This tender exchange of ideas happened only an hour or so after the robbery, and there was plenty of excitement around about that. But Sam went soberly about his work as telephone lineman. Rosie simply rode with him as a – well, it wasn't as a bodyguard, but a sort of M.P. escort – Morals Police.

It was good fortune that he'd been in Dunnsville when the robbery happened, because his prompt repair of the phone wires had spoiled the robbers' getaway plans. They hadn't gotten ten miles from Dunnsville before somebody fired a load of buckshot at them as their car roared past Lemons' Store. They were past before they realized they'd been shot at. But the buckshot had punctured the radiator, and two miles on they were stuck. They pushed their car off the road behind some bushes and struck out on foot, and the sheriff ran smack past their car without seeing it. Then rain began to fall, and the bank robbers were wet and scared and desperate. They knew there'd be roadblocks set up everywhere, and they had that bag of money – part of it bills but a lot of it silver – and all of Tidewater was up in arms.

They took evasive action. They hastily stuffed their pockets with small bills – there were no big ones – but dared not take too much lest they bulge. They hid the major part of their loot in a hollow tree. They separated, fast. One of them got on the Batesville-to-Rappahannock bus and disappeared that way. The other two stole a rowboat and got across the Severn. All of them went to nearby towns – while rain fell heavily and covered their trails – and went to bed with chest-colds from their wetting. They felt miserable. But the rain washed away the scent they'd left, and bloodhounds couldn't do a thing.

None of this meant anything yet to Sam. Rosie had taken charge of him, and she kept charge. She rode with him all the afternoon of the robbery. When quitting time came he took her home and prepared to retire from the scene.

But she said grimly, 'Oh, no you don't! You're staying right here! You're going to sleep in my brother's room, and my pa is going to put a padlock on the door so you don't go roaming off to call up that no-account other you and get in more trouble!'

Sam said uneasily, 'I might mess things up if I don't talk to him.'

'He's messed things up enough talking to you!' Rosie said. 'The idea of repeating our private affairs! He hadn't ought to know them! And I'm not sure,' she said ominously, 'that you didn't tell him! If you did, Sam Yoder—'

Sam didn't argue that point. There was no argument to make. He was practically meek until he discovered after supper that the schedule for the evening was a thrilling game of cribbage played in the living room where Rosie's mother and father were. He mentioned unhappily that they were acting like old married people without the fun of getting that way, but he said that only once. Rosie glared at him. And when bedtime came she shooed him into her brother's room and her father padlocked him in. He did not sleep well. Next morning, there was Rosie in her blue jeans with a monkey wrench in her pocket, ready to go riding with him. She did. And the next day. And the next. And the next. Nothing happened. The state banking association put up five thousand dollars' reward for the bank robbers, and the insurance company put up some more, but there wasn't a trace of the criminals.

There wasn't a trace of criminality about Sam, either. Rosie rode with him, but there wasn't any love-making. They exchanged not one single hand-squeeze, nor one melting glance, nor did they even play footsie while they were eating lunch in the truck outside a filling station. Their conduct was exemplary, and it wore on Sam. Possibly it wore on Rosie, too.

Once Sam said morosely, as he chewed on a ham sandwich at lunchtime, 'Rosie, I'm crazy about you, but this feels like I've been divorced without ever even getting married first.'

And Rosie snapped, 'If I told you how I feel, that other you in the week after next would laugh his fool head off. So shut up!'

Things were bad, and they got no better. For nearly a week Rosie rode everywhere with Sam, in Sam's truck. Their conduct was exemplary. They acted in a manner that Rosie's parents would in theory have approved, but which they didn't even begin to believe in. They did nothing the world could not have watched without their being embarrassed, and they said very little that all the world would not have been bored to hear.

It must have been the eleventh of July when they almost snapped at each other and Rosie said bitterly, 'Let me drive a while. I need to have to put my mind on something that it don't make me mad to think about.'

'Go ahead,' Sam said gloomily. He stopped the truck and got out the door. 'I don't look for any happiness in this world any more, anyways.'

He went around to the other side of the truck while she slid to the driver's seat.

She said, 'Tomorrow's going to be the twelfth. Do you realize it?'

'It'll be the twelfth,' Sam admitted. 'But what's the difference?'

'That's the day,' said Rosie, 'where the other you was when he called you up the first time.'

'That's right,' said Sam morbidly. 'It is.'

'And so far,' said Rosie, jamming her foot down on the accelerator viciously, 'I've kept you honest. If you change into a scoundrel between now and tomorrow—'

She changed to second gear. The truck jerked and bounced.

'Hey!' said Sam. 'Watch your driving!'

'Don't you tell me how to drive, Sam Yoder!' snapped Rosie.

'But if I get killed before tomorrow—'

Rosie changed gear again – too soon. The truck bucked, so she jammed down the accelerator again, and it almost leaped off the road.

'If you get killed before tomorrow,' raged Rosie, infuriated because of innumerable things and the misbehavior of the truck on top of the rest. 'If you get killed before tomorrow, it'll serve you right! I've been thinking and thinking and thinking. And – even if I stop you from being a crook, there'll always be that – other you, knowing everything we say and do—' She was hitting forty miles an hour and the speed was still going up. 'So there'd still be no use – no hope anyway—'

She sobbed, partly in rage and partly in despair. The roadway curved sharply just about there, and she swung the truck crazily around it – and there was a car standing only halfway off the road. Sam grabbed for the steering wheel, but there wasn't time. The light half-truck, still accelerating, hit the parked car with the noise of dozens of empty oil drums falling downstairs. The truck was slued halfway around and bounced back, and then it charged forward and slammed into the parked car a second time. Then it stalled.

Somebody yelled at Sam. He got out of the truck, looked at the damage and tried to figure out how it was that neither he nor Rosie had been killed. Then he tried despairingly to think how he was going to explain to the telephone company that he'd let Rosie drive.

The voice yelled louder. Right at the edge of the woodland there was a reddish-haired character screaming at him and tugging at his hip pocket. The words he used were not fit for Rosie's shell-like ears – even if they did probably come near matching the way she felt. The reddish-haired man said more naughty words at the top of his voice. His hand came away from his hip pocket with something glittering in it.

Sam was swinging when the glitter began, and he connected before the pistol bore. There was a sort of squashy smacking sound, and the reddish-haired man lay down in the road and was still.

'Migawd!' said Sam blankly. 'This was the fella in front of the bank! He's one of those bank robbers!'

He stared. There was a loud crashing in the brushwood. The accident had happened at the edge of some woodland, and Sam did not need a high IQ to know that the friends of the red-haired man must be on the way. A second later he saw them. Rosie was just getting out of the car then. She was very pale, and there wasn't time to tell her to get started up if possible and away from there. One of the two running men was carrying a canvas bag with the words *Bank of Dunnsville* on it. They came for Sam. As they came they expressed opinions of the state of things, of Sam, of the cosmos – of everything but the weather – in terms even more reprehensible than the first man had used.

They saw the reddish-haired man lying down on the ground. One of them – he'd come out into the road behind the truck and was running for Sam – jerked out a pistol. He was in the act of raising it to use it on Sam at a range of something like six feet when there was a peculiar noise behind him. It was a sort of hollow *clunk*! That even at such a time needed to have attention paid to it. The man jerked his head around to see.

And the *clunk*! had been made by Rosie's monkey wrench, falling imperatively on the head of another man who had come out of the woods. She had carried it to use on Sam. She used it on a total stranger. He fell down and lay peacefully still.

Then Sam swung a second time, on the man behind him.

Then there was silence, save for the sweet singing of birds among the trees and the whirrings and other insect noises of creatures in the grass and brushwood.

Presently there were other noises, but they were made by Rosie. She wept, hanging onto Sam.

He unwound her arms from around his neck, went thoughtfully to the back of the truck and got some phone wire and his pliers. He fastened the men's hands together behind them, and then he tied their feet. He piled the three bank robbers in the back of the light truck together with the money they had stolen.

Presently they came to, one by one, and Rosie and Sam explained severely that they must watch their language in the presence of a lady. But the three seemed so dazed by what had befallen them that Sam and Rosie didn't have much trouble.

Rosie's parents would have been pleased at how completely proper their behavior was while they took the three bank robbers into town and turned them over to the sheriff. Rosie's parents would also have been surprised.

That night Rosie sat out on the porch with Sam, and they discussed the particular events of the day in some detail. But Rosie was still cagey about the other Sam. So Sam decided to assert himself.

About half-past nine he said firmly, 'Well then, Rosie, I guess I'd better be getting along home. I've got to try one more time to call myself up on the telephone and tell me to mind my own business.'

'Says who?' said Rosie grimly. 'Oh, no you're not! You're staying locked up right here tonight, and I'm riding with you tomorrow. If I kept you honest this far, I can keep it up till sundown tomorrow! Then maybe it'll stick!'

Sam protested, but it didn't work. Rosie was adamant. Not only about keeping him from being a crook, but from having any fun to justify his virtue. She shooed him into her brother's room, and her father locked him in. Sam did not sleep very well, because it looked like virtue wasn't even its own reward and the future looked dark indeed. He sat up, brooding. It must have been close to dawn when the obvious hit him like a ton of bricks.

Then he gazed blankly at the wall and said, 'Migawd! O'course!'

He grinned, all by himself, as though he would split his throat. And at breakfast he practically sang as he stuffed himself with pancakes and syrup, and Rosie's utterly depressed expression changed to one of baffled despair.

He smiled tenderly upon her when she came doggedly out to the truck in her blue jeans and with the monkey wrench in her pocket. They started off just like any other day and he said amiably, 'Rosie, the sheriff says we get five thousand dollars reward from the bankers' association, and there's more from the insurance company, and there's odd bits of change due for rewards specially offered for those fellas for past performances. We're going to be right well off.'

Rosie looked at him gloomily. There was still the matter of the other Sam in the middle of the week after next. And just then Sam – who had been watching the telephone-lines beside the road as he drove – pulled off the road and put on his climbing-irons.

'What's this?' asked Rosie mournfully. 'You know—'

'You listen,' said Sam happily.

He climbed zestfully to the top of the pole. He hooked in the little gadget that didn't make private conversations possible on a party line, but did make it possible for a man to talk to himself two weeks in the future.

Or the past.

'Hello!' said Sam, up at the top of the telephone pole. 'Sam, this is you.'

A voice he knew perfectly well sounded in the receiver.

'Huh? Who's that?'

'This is you,' said Sam. 'You, Sam Yoder. Don't you recognize your own voice? This is you, Sam Yoder, calling from the twelfth of July. Don't hang up!'

He heard Rosie gasp, all the way down there in the banged-up telephone-truck. Sam had seen the self-evident at last, and now, on the twelfth of July, he was talking to himself on the telephone. Only instead of talking to himself in the week after next, he was now talking to himself in the week before last – he being back there ten days before, working on the very same telephone-line on this very same pole. And it was the same conversation, word for word.

When he came down the pole, rather expansively, Rosie clung to him weeping.

'Oh, Sam!' she sobbed. 'It was you all the time! Only you!'

'Yeah,' said Sam complacently. 'I figured it out last night. That me back there in the second of July, he's cussing me out. And he's going to tell you about it, and you're going to get all wrought up. But I can make that dumb me back yonder do what has to be done. And you and me, Rosie, have got a lot of money coming to us. I'm going to carry on through so he'll earn it for us. But I'm warning you, Rosie, he'll be back at my house waiting for me to talk to him tonight, and I've got to be home to tell him to go over to your house. I'm goin' to say ha ha, ha ha at him.'

'A-all right,' said Rosie, wide-eyed. 'You can.'

'But,' said Sam. 'I remember that when I call me up tonight, back there ten days ago, I'm going to be right busy here and now tonight. I'm going to make me mad, because I don't want to waste time talking to myself back yonder. Remember?' Then Rosie turned red. 'Now what would I be doing tonight that makes me not want to waste time talking to myself ten days ago?' Sam asked mildly. 'You got any ideas, Rosie?'

'Sam Yoder!' Rosie said. 'I won't! I wouldn't! I never heard of such a thing!'

Sam looked at her and shook his head regretfully.

'Too bad! If you won't, I guess I've got to call me up in the week after next and find out what's cooking.'

'You – you shan't!' said Rosie fiercely. 'You, Sam Yoder – I'll get even with you! But you shan't talk to that—' Then she wailed. 'Doggone you, Sam! Even if I do have to marry you so you'll be wanting to talk to that dumb you ten days back, you're not going to – you're not—'

Sam grinned. He kissed her. He put her in the truck and they rode off to Batesville to get married. And they did.

But as you're not supposed to believe all this, and if you ask Sam Yoder about it, he's apt to say that it's all a lie. He doesn't want the question of privacy raised again. And there are other matters. For instance, Sam's getting to be a pretty prominent citizen these days. He makes a lot of money, one way and another. Nobody around home will ever bet with him on who's going to win a baseball game, anyhow.

THE DEVIL OF EAST LUPTON

Occult? Very definitely not. As far as records show, Leinster never wrote in this genre *– although sometimes it seemed as if he was going to (as in 'The Power'). No, the following is very definitely hard-line SF, very pleasantly laced with humor. Not that Mr. Tedder found the situation very funny . . . .*

To this day nobody pretends to understand the Devil of East Lupton, Vermont. There are even differences of opinion about the end to which that devil came. Mr. Tedder is sure he was the fiend in question, and that he ceased to be fiendish when he rid himself of the pot over his head.

Other authorities believe that heavy ordnance did the trick, and point to a quarter-mile crater for proof. It takes close reasoning to decide.

But if by the Devil of East Lupton you mean the Whatever-it-was that came out of Somewhere to Here, and caused all the catastrophes by his mere arrival – why – then the Devil was the Whatever-it-was in the leathery, hidelike covering on the morning Mr. Tedder ran away from the constable.

On that morning, Mr. Tedder ran like a deer – or as nearly like a deer as Mr. Tedder could hope to run. The resemblance was not close. Deer do not hesitate helplessly between possible avenues of escape. Deer do not plunge out of concealing thickets to scuttle through merely shoulder-high brush because a pathway shows. But Mr. Tedder did.

The constable, behind him, shouted wrathfully. There was a thirty-day jail-sentence waiting for someone for vagrancy – which is to say, for not having any money. Mr. Tedder was elected.

He would not gain any money by staying in jail, but the

constable who arrested him and the justice of the peace who sentenced him would receive fees for their activity. That was why this township was notoriously a bad place for tramps, bums, blanket-stiffs and itinerant workmen in need of a job.

'I can't go much further,' Mr. Tedder thought. His heart thumped horribly. There was an agonizing stitch in his side. His breath was a hoarse, honking noise as it rushed in and out. Despair filled him as exhaustion neared.

He pounded, sobbing for breath, up a little ten-foot rise. His eyes tried to blur with tears. Then he lurched down the other side of the ridge and saw that he was in the neglected, broken-limbed orchard of an abandoned farm.

The house was partly collapsed and wholly ruined. A remaining shed leaned crazily. Vines climbed over a rail fence – three parts rotten – and went on along a strand of barbed wire nailed to tree-trunks.

He could run no further. He looked, despairing, for a hiding place. His haggard, ineffectual face turned desperately. He saw something dark and large. To his blurred eyes it looked like a cow. He ran toward it. It shrank back, stirring. . . .

There was a thin, high screaming noise, like gas escaping through a punctured tire, but a tire inflated to a monstrous pressure. There was a vast, foggy vaporousness. The dark shape made convulsive movements, but Mr. Tedder was too lost in panic to take note. He ran blindly toward it.

'Ug!' gasped Mr. Tedder.

The scream descended in pitch. A pungent, ammoniacal smell filled the air. Mr. Tedder ran into a wisp of fog which tore at his lungs. He choked and fell – which was fortunate, because the air was clearer near the ground. He lay kicking among dead leaves and dry grass-stems while a gray vapor spread and spread, and a very gentle breeze urged it sidewise among the unkempt trees of the orchard.

The noise died away in a long-continued moan which included gurglings. It still sounded like gas escaping from very high pressure.

The gurglings were like spoutings of liquid within.

But Mr. Tedder was in no mood to analyze. He had been

breathless to begin with. He had been strangled on top of that. Now he writhed in the dry grass, ready to sob because the constable would presently lay hands on him and haul him to jail.

He heard the constable shout again, furiously. Then Mr. Tedder heard him cough. The constable bellowed, 'Fire!' and fled.

He ran into a tendril of wispy, creeping vapor which did look a lot like smoke. He fell down, strangling. Again the air was clearer among the tangled stalks of frost-killed grasses. The constable coughed and wheezed.

Presently he staggered away to report that a vagabond had set fire to the woods to hinder pursuit. But there was no fire. The chill vapor which looked like smoke very gradually dissipated. A cursory glance would send the firefighters home again.

Mr. Tedder lay sobbing and gasping on the ground, expecting at any instant to be seized. He panted in despair. But the constable did not reappear. He never returned. Mr. Tedder was alone, his escape good.

When he realized it, he sat up abruptly. His meek face expressed astonishment. He stared all about him. There was still a small space from which an ever-thinner gray vapor seeped away. There was a reek as of ammonia in the air – a highly improbable smell around an abandoned farmhouse.

Presently Mr. Tedder got to his feet. He brushed off the leaves and grass-stems which clung to his shabby garments. He was a few yards from a distinctly tumbledown woodshed and almost under a gnarled apple-tree to which a few leaves still clung, and where he could observe a single, dried-up apple clinging tenaciously to its parent bough.

The sight of the apple gave him pause. He hunted busily. He found windfalls. Untended, the apples would be wormy and small and belated at best. But Mr. Tedder had learned not to be over-fastidious. He found a dozen or more scrubby objects which were partly eatable. He ate them.

It was then that he heard a bubbling noise, like something boiling in a pot. The sounds came from the place where the gray mist rose. He went to the spot, and wrinkled his nose. The smell of ammonia was stronger. It seemed to come from a collapsed object on the ground which was remotely like a deflated hide. A liquid came from a small rent in it and bubbled furiously to nothingness.

A student of physics would have said that it had an extraordinarily low boiling-point, like a liquefied gas. Mr. Tedder said nothing. He regarded the flaccid skin-like thing surprisedly. He had seen it a little while since, inflated and moving about.

There must have been something inside it to move it.

Mr. Tedder could see, of course, where it had a tiny tear. It had moved or been moved back against a single strand of barbed wire, hidden among vine-stems. It had punctured, and there it was. But Mr. Tedder could never have imagined a creature which required an extremely cold gas like ammonia and hydrogen, mixed, at extremely high pressure, in order to live. He could not have conceived of such a creature wearing a flexible garment to contain that high-pressure, low-temperature gas for it to breathe. Assuredly he would never envision anything, beast or devil, which at released pressure and the temperature of a Vermont autumn day would melt to liquid and boil away to nothing.

'It don't make sense,' he muttered, scratching his unkempt head.

So Mr. Tedder, who could not think comprehendingly, did not think at all. He saw something on the ground – no, two things. They were metal, and they smouldered and smoked like the flat thing, because they were cold. They were unbelievably cold. One looked like an aluminum pot. But pots do not have chilly linked-metal straps in the place of handles, nor hemispherical knobs, a good inch and a half in diameter, on one rim. The other object looked like a gun. Not a real gun, of course. But vaguely, approximately, like a gun just the same.

He picked up the pot. It was all of an inch and a half thick. It was very light for such a thickness. Mr. Tedder cheered suddenly. It was undoubtedly aluminum. There is a market for scrap aluminum. East Lupton was out of bounds, of course, but there might be a junk-dealer in South Lupton. This ought to be worth fifty cents, and he might get a quarter for it.

'Two bits is still two bits,' he thought.

He touched the other thing gingerly. It was still bitterly cold, but the frost melted under the warmth of his finger. It would weigh fifteen pounds or so. Another twenty-five cents. . . .

Mr. Tedder marched on happily. Then he came upon broken branches, freshly crushed down from trees. He saw another gray mist before him. He approached it cautiously. He saw where something had crashed down through the trees and knocked off the top of a six-inch maple. He pushed on inquisitively. . . .

The thing had ploughed into soft earth and almost buried itself. A foot-thick tree was splintered and had crashed to cover the object that had broken it. Mr. Tedder saw whiteness through the toppled branches. It seemed to be a sphere not much over ten feet in diameter, and it was completely covered with frost. A chilly mist oozed away from it. Mr. Tedder stared at it with the metal pot in one hand and the gun – if it was a gun – in the other.

There was silence save for the faintly sibilant whispering of the trees overhead. There was the lurid coloring of Vermont in the fall. A bird called somewhere, a long distance away. Then Mr. Tedder heard a motor running. It sounded very queer.

'*Thud-thud-thud-thud-CHUNK! Thud-thud-thud-thud-CHUNK!*' It was running in the frost-covered sphere under the fallen tree.

'I'll be darned!' he said aloud.

It occurred vaguely to Mr. Tedder that this and the deflated object back yonder were somehow connected. He picked his way cautiously around the smashed branches and shattered trees. Well away, he felt cheerful because he had escaped the law and picked up salable junk. The two objects were pretty heavy, too. The pot would fit on his head, though, and would be easier to carry so. He put it over his battered soft hat and drew the chain-link strap under his chin. Then he examined the thing like a gun. There was a knob on one side, an inch and a half in diameter. He tugged at it.

There was a sharp buzzing sound. Something that looked like flame came out of the end. It spread out in a precisely shaped, mathematically perfect cone, and blotted out brush-wood, trees – everything.

Mr. Tedder jerked the knob back, startled, on the first sounding of the noise. The flame-like appearance lasted less than half a second. But where the flame had played upon foliage and brush there wasn't anything left. Nothing at all but a little fine ash, sifting down towards earth. And the grass and top-soil were eaten away as if a virulent acid had been spilled over them.

Mr. Tedder stood frozen for the tenth part of a heartbeat. Then in one motion he threw away the gun and fled. The pot flopped down over his eyes, blinding him. He hit his head a terrific blow against a low-hanging limb. Instantly, it seemed to him, the chain-link strap tightened. He went almost mad with terror. But when he got the pot back so he could see, he fled with the heavy thing bobbing and bumping on his head.

Presently his own panting slowed him down. He remembered the knob on the rim of the pot. He stopped and fumbled with it. It came off in his hand with a crystalline fracture to show where it had broken in his first collision. He couldn't get the pot off.

He worked for a long time, sweating in something close to hysterical panic. He was terrified of the thing he had thrown away, and by transference, of the pot on his head. He desired passionately to be rid of it. He felt a sort of poignant desperation. But he would have to get somebody to cut the strap in order to be freed.

He came to the edge of the thicket beyond East Lupton. He looked out upon rolling country, undulating to the mountain's foot. There was a cluster of houses in the distance. Still terrified, and with the pot bumping on his head, Mr. Tedder struck out for the village.

He saw a tiny bundle of fur in his way. It was a dead rabbit. He passed on. He saw, very far ahead, a white dog running from a farmhouse to intercept him. But Mr. Tedder was not afraid of dogs. He was afraid of the pot on his head. Presently he saw the dog no more than ten feet away. It lay sprawled out, motionless. It looked dead. Then he saw the throb-throb of a heartbeat. It was asleep, or unconscious. He hastened on.

He came to the highway and ran toward a wagon for help. And there was a horse lying down between the shafts. The man in the wagon, too, had sagged limply. Both were alive, but both were unconscious.

'Something screwy here,' he thought.

Mr. Tedder had his own terror, but this was an emergency even more immediate than his own. He tried to help the man. He did get him down to the road, and laid him solicitously on the dead-grass bank by the side of the road. He loosened his clothing and went on toward the village at a run to summon help. Afterward he would get the pot off his head.

But the village was unconscious, too, when he got there. Male and female, man, woman, child, and beast, the inhabitants of South Lupton lay in crumpled heaps.

He saw a small boy unconscious over a toy wagon. A woman had collapsed into a laundry-basket beside a clothes-line. A little farther on, a mule lay with its legs spraddled absurdly. Then he saw two men flung headlong as if they had been running when weakness overtook them. It began to look as if alarm had come to the village.

People had thronged out of their houses to fall in heaps on the sidewalk, at their doors – everywhere. He saw a car that had run into a gas-pump, and just beyond another car which had run off the road and stalled on a hillside. Dogs, cats, chickens – the very pigeons and crows lay motionless on the ground.

Mr. Tedder felt a horrible panic, and the pot on his head bumped him, but he tried desperately to rise to the emergency this situation constituted. He tried to rouse the unconscious people lying in the street. He loosened clothing, he sprinkled water, he chafed hands – to no avail. His meek, normally apprehensive features went consciously stern and resolute.

Presently he tried to summon help by telephone, but there was a local exchange and the operator lay unconscious in her chair. In the end, and in desperation, Mr. Tedder commandeered a bicycle on which to seek aid.

The essential rightness of his character was shown by the fact that he rifled no purses. He looted nothing. The Bank of South Lupton lay open to him, and it did not occur to him to fill his pockets. He got on a bicycle and rode off like mad, the absurd pot bobbing on his head as he pedaled.

He came to a car that had smashed into a ditch and turned over. Flames licked at its gasoline-tank. Mr. Tedder leaped off the bicycle and dragged out an unconscious man and a little girl. He hauled them to safety and tried to put out the fire. He failed.

He pedaled on madly in quest of a doctor, when attempts to rouse these two people failed as had all the rest. He was in a new panic now, somehow. He remembered, though vaguely, talk of a broadcast of years before concerning the landing of Martians upon the earth. Mr. Tedder was not quite sure whether Martians had landed or not, but somehow it suddenly frightened him to remember the frost covered globe which had smashed trees in landing.

'You'd think I was Orson Welles or somebody,' he gulped.

He reached the town of West Lupton. The names of towns in Vermont are not good evidence of Yankee ingenuity. The town itself was a tiny place of five hundred people. As he pedaled into it, it looked like the scene of a massacre. Its inhabitants lay unconscious everywhere. There were not even flies in the air.

Mr. Tedder did not give up for two full hours, during which he pedaled desperately in quest of some other conscious human being. By now his fear had come to be for himself, and it grew until it made him almost unaware of the ill-fitting, bumping pot upon his head. But at long last his teeth chattered.

'M-maybe,' said Mr. Tedder quaveringly to himself, 'I'm the only man left alive in these parts . . .'

With the terror came an impulse to hide. It was then late afternoon. It would soon be dark. He did not want to be in a town filled with still, not-dead forms after dark! He pedaled down a side road. It became a cart-track and climbed. It dwindled to a footpath. He dived into the obscurity of woodland as the shadows grew deep.

He came at last to an empty, rocky hilltop. Sunset was over.

Only a lingering dim red glow remained in the west. Presently stars shone down. He looked up at them, sweating.

If that frost-covered thing had come from the stars, something from it – a sort of devil – had stricken down the hundreds of unconscious people Mr. Tedder had seen. Maybe it was getting ready for more of its kind. He stared upward and imagined other spheres swinging down out of the darkness overhead to gouge long furrows in the ground. Maybe such things were falling all over the world....

But he could look across-country for miles. Presently he saw joyfully that there were electric lights. He saw motorcar headlights on the highways. In particular, he saw that the very last town he had entered was now brightly lighted and there was traffic moving in and out....

'Well,' he thought with relief. 'Whatever it was, it ain't permanent.' Come morning he would have somebody cut loose the pot from his head.

He could not find fuel to make a fire, but he snatched some fitful sleep toward dawn. He was bitterly cold when he woke, and at earliest daylight he made his way back toward town.

The dawn light was still gray and dreary when he reached it. The streets were empty. But there was a motor-truck stopped by a store, its motor purring. And there was a man tumbled in a heap above a bunch of big-city newspapers he had just put out of the truck for delivery. The man was alive, but unconscious. There was a cat in a motionless furry heap beside him, as if it had come out to rub against his legs and had collapsed without warning.

Mr. Tedder, shivering, turned the man over. He was insensible. He could not be roused. Mr. Tedder felt hysteria stirring within him. The pot hurt his head, now. The places where it rubbed most often were getting sore. Then he noticed the headlines.

DISASTER IN VERMONT – DEVIL
LOOSE, SAY VILLAGERS

Unexplained Mass Unconsciousness Strikes Countryside

In the gray twilight of dawn, with a softly purring truck behind him and before him an unconscious man, Mr. Tedder read.

'South Lupton struck by strange, creeping unconsciousness that moved like a wall or an invisible flood of oblivion. ... Entire villages insensible for half an hour. ... Some inhabitants undisturbed where they fell, others hauled about and pawed, but unharmed. ... The same inexplicable insensibility moved along roads. ... Man driving with his little daughter lost consciousness and came to to find his car overturned and burning, and himself and the little girl lying some distance away. ... Farmers found their horses struggling up from unconsciousness. ...'

Mr. Tedder's throat went dry. He looked around furtively. This town had borne the look of a shambles yesterday, when he was here. From the hilltop he had seen it alive. But now it was dead again. ... Suddenly he remembered a white dog that had come running toward him across a wide pasture. When he got to the dog it was unconscious. ...

'I wonder if ...' He could not face the thought.

Mr. Tedder shivered. He almost whimpered. But after a little he picked up the unconscious man before him. He dragged him into the back of the truck. He drove clumsily and unaccustomedly out of the town. There was a long, straight stretch of road. Mr. Tedder went well out upon it. He stopped and let the unconscious man carefully down to the side of the road. He got back in the driver's seat and drove away. He watched through the back-view mirror.

When he was a little more than half a mile away, the still figure stirred, rolled over, and got dazedly upright.

Mr. Tedder swallowed noisily. He drove on a little way and found a place where he could turn. He headed back. The owner of the truck still stood bewildered in the road. Mr. Tedder drove toward him. When he was still half a mile away, the man crumpled up and lay in a heap on the road. He was a flaccid, limp, insensible figure when Mr. Tedder brought the truck to a stop and loaded him in again.

He turned once more and rode on toward South Lupton. Mr.

Tedder's face was a sickly gray color. The meekness of his normal expression was replaced by an odd, fixed horror. He had found two things which he believed came from the frosted ten-foot sphere. One was a weapon which destroyed everything when a knob on its side was touched. The other was this pot, with a strap which now held it fast upon his head.

The pot was a weapon too. It did not affect the one who wore it. The tightening of the strap when it went on was to make sure – pure anguish sharpened Mr. Tedder's perceptions – that it could not fall off while it was operating. If it did, the person – or the devil – wearing it would fall a victim too. It did not fit a man because it was designed for the brain-case of something else, something Mr. Tedder had seen vaguely as a dark moving object backing into a rusty barbed wire strung between two trees. If the pot – or helmet – had been turned on then, Mr. Tedder would never have seen anything. He would have fallen unconscious a half-mile away. . . .

He made a little sobbing noise in his throat. He drove unskillfully to South Lupton. One general store was open. He went into it and filled his pockets with canned food, a loaf of bread, and matches. He took two blankets from a shelf. He stepped carefully over the two clerks and four customers in the store. They were on the floor, of course. He walked out of the store and away from the little town.

'I got to get back there,' he said unsteadily. 'I got to!'

A long while later he strode across rolling pasture-land. A white dog ran to intercept him. He saw it as a distant white speck. When he came up to it, it was a still, senseless heap. He went on to the woods and into them. It took him two hours to find the gash blasted in the woods by the gun-like thing. Then it took him another half-hour to find the gun.

He shivered when he picked it up, and carried it gingerly, but he noted that the metal was deeply pitted now. On the side that was next to the damp earth, the metal was eaten away to a depth of a quarter of an inch or more.

He found the abandoned orchard, and the half-collapsed and wholly ruined house. Then he sat down and stared dully at nothing, trying to think of a solution to his predicament.

Night fell but he sat in a sort of lethargy of despair for a long while. Ultimately he rolled up in the blankets. The pot on his head was horribly uncomfortable. It had not been made for a human head, and it did not fit. Twice during the night, also, he woke with a feeling of strangulation. He had stirred in his sleep and the tight chin-strap had choked him. The second time he found himself close to the metal gun. He had almost touched it. He made an inarticulate sound, such as a man might make who found himself about to step on a rattlesnake.

He got up and found the well of the abandoned farm. He dropped a clod of earth in it. It splashed. He dropped in the gun like-thing. Bubbling sounds followed. They lasted a long time.

He stayed at the abandoned farm for three days living on the canned stuff he had taken. His cheeks grew sunken and his eyes querulously pathetic. Also, a sore place started from the rubbing of the pot on his head. On the second day he found the frosted globe again. The motor in it still ran. '*Thud-thud-thud-thud-CHUNK! Thud-thud-thud-thud-CHUNK!*' There was no sign that anything had come out. Perhaps there had only been one Whatever-it-was in it, and that had succumbed to a rip in its artificial hide by a bit of barbed wire. No trace of that thing remained, now. It had evaporated.

'Jellyfish. Like jellyfish,' he told himself.

Mr. Tedder did not think in scientific terms nor speculate from what planet or star the Whatever-it-was had come. If he had been told that on the planet Jupiter there was atmosphere of ammonia and hydrogen under enormous pressure, it would have meant nothing to him. The suggestion that the specific gravity of the giant planet meant that only light metals like sodium, potassium, and lithium – all interacting readily with water – could exist there . . . Such a suggestion would have had exactly no meaning at all.

His mind dwelt exclusively upon the fact that any human being who came within a half-mile of him must fall unconscious and remain so. To the human race he was a menace; a devil. And that if he should manage to get the thick and clumsy pot off his head, he too would fall unconscious and remain so.

He was in the most horrible solitary confinement imaginable.

He was invulnerable, to be sure. He could rob with impunity and do murder without fear of any penalty. But nobody could speak to him. Ever.

On the fourth day he went into East Lupton for food.

On the fifth day aeroplanes flew overhead, back and forth. One suddenly went spinning, out of control, dipping down toward the treetops. It recovered, a bare few hundred feet up and three-quarters of a mile away. The planes disappeared.

On the sixth day bombs fell. The first racking explosions terrified him incomparably. He fled through the underbrush. He came out of it and saw soldiers. They made a cordon about an area of woodland probably two miles square. They toppled in unconscious heaps as Mr. Tedder drew near them, and as if that were a signal there were distant boomings and artillery shells fell close to where he peered out. Mr. Tedder ran away. He dodged shells and bombs until night fell, then he ran, weeping bitterly to himself.

'I ain't done nothing wrong!' the thought beat through his imprisoned head.

Of course the troops could not stop him. He pelted through their lines, unheeding. Presently he reached the village of East Lupton. No figures moved in it. Desperate, he entered it. There were many soldiers among the heaps of shallow-breathing, staring-eyed folk who lay slackly wherever unconsciousness had overtaken them.

Mr. Tedder found food, and wolfed it. The store in which he found it was a country-village general store and sold everything. Mr. Tedder was half-mad now. The thing he wore was an intolerable burden. One of the sore places on his head from its rubbing was excruciatingly painful. It was infected. Other sore places were developing. And he was a sort of devil, working havoc wherever he moved. He took weapons – for which he had no need – and metal-cutting tools he would not dare to use. . . . And he saw newspapers.

GUNS TO BLAST DEVIL OF
EAST LUPTON

He read the news account. The one-mile circle of insensibility had been deduced. Its cause was not understood, but it was certain that some sensate thing was its center. It moved. It had made definite travels and returned to its starting-point. Troops now cordoned the place where it nested restlessly, and artillery was being massed. A barrage that nothing could survive would presently be poured in. . . .

Mr. Tedder looked at a powerful, sleek car. He could take it and go anywhere, and all of humanity was powerless to stop him – or to help him. Anyone who came near him would fall senseless. Even he, if he took off the thing on his head. . . .

A motor-truck came rolling into the village, its driver stricken unconscious at the wheel. It seemed certain to roll on and on.

Mr. Tedder screamed at it. But something deflected its wheels. It curved sedately from the highway and ploughed across a sidewalk and crashed into the corner of a house.

When the sun rose, Mr. Tedder was back at the abandoned farm which for no reason at all he considered his headquarters. His eyes were red with bitter weeping. His meek expression was utterly woebegone. But his determination was made.

Great bombers roared high overhead, so high they were mere specks. Things dropped from them. Boomings began, all around the horizon. Shells struck and blasted. The tumult, once begun, was unending.

Mr. Tedder cringed. Shaken and battered, he filed at the chain-link strap which held the pot on his head. The metal was soft, but the links shifted under his fingers, which trembled uncontrollably.

A shell burst fifty yards away. Mr. Tedder was moved to sheer hysteria. He could do no such fine work as filing. He took the snips he had appropriated the night before. Once the thing was off his head, he would know nothing; no terror, no pain; nothing at all. The pot which had ridden him like the Old Man of the Sea would kill him. But he wanted to be rid of it. He did not want to be near it even in death. 'Just get it off me!' he shouted. He was a little mad now.

The earth shook under him. Blast-waves beat at him. Half-deafened, sobbing, he crawled to the well. He pulled at the rotten boards. He hung his head over the noisome depth. He used the metal-snips – he had trouble getting them under the chain-link strap – to chew at the soft metal. The earth trembled under concussions. Bits of loose earth and rotted wood tumbled into the well from its edges.

The snips met triumphantly. . . . The pot tumbled down into the well and floated for a moment, rocking. Then it tilted and filled and sank. A thin, scummy veil of bubbles arose. Some light metals react readily with water. Potassium violently, sodium freely, lithium readily. The pot was of an alloy which would be highly useful where it was permanently too cold for water ever to turn liquid. But on earth . . .

Mr. Tedder sat up. He felt giddy; light-headed; incredibly relieved. But a shell fell thirty yards away, and a bomb exploded horribly just over the ridge, and something ripped through the half-collapsed house and exploded on beyond. There had been a devil in this woods. The devil of East Lupton, Vermont. The artillery searched for it, to exorcise it, but Mr. Tedder was not unconscious.

'It's gone!' he cried joyfully. 'And I'm okay now.'

It would never occur to him that designers of a weapon who planned for the tightening of a fastening-strap when it was turned on, so that it could not possibly make its own wearer a victim, would also arrange for it to be turned off if the fastening-strap should be broken or cut. It would be the most obvious of safety devices.

But Mr. Tedder's intellectual processes would never grasp such a thing. He simply knew that he was not unconscious and that the bombardment went on. It was overwhelming. It was maddening. Mr. Tedder put his hands over his ears and wept, cringing to the earth and awaiting death.

Then the earth seemed to buckle beneath him. It raised up and dealt him a violent blow. Over where the frosted sphere lay self-buried in the ground, there was a sudden, incredible, impossible flare. A shell had hit the enigmatic globe in which an untended motor had run so long. The sphere exploded.

The violence of the explosion suggested power much greater than anything human. The fuel-store of the sphere must have detonated. It made a crater a quarter-mile across, and every least fragment of the sphere itself was atomized and destroyed.

The explosion seemed to the military to mark the death of something spectacular. They stopped the barrage and explosions.

They found Mr. Tedder unconscious. He was sleeping as if drugged, from reaction to the end of strain. Near him there was a caved-in well which, of course, was not worth digging out.

It was assumed that Mr. Tedder had remained unconscious through all the career of the Devil of East Lupton, Vermont. He was hospitalized, and kindly told what had happened, and ultimately turned loose with a new suit of clothes and a five-dollar bill. And Mr. Tedder disappeared into the vast obscurity of the world of tramps, bums, blanket-stiffs and itinerant workmen.

And to this day nobody pretends that they really understood anything about the Devil of East Lupton, Vermont. There are even marked differences of opinion concerning its ending. Mr. Tedder thinks he was the Devil, and that he somehow ceased to be fiendish when he got the pot off his head. Other authorities think that heavy ordnance destroyed the Devil, and point to a quarter-mile crater as proof.

But if by the Devil of East Lupton you mean the Whatever-it-was that came out of the Somewhere into the Here and caused all the catastrophes by his mere arrival. . . . Why, in that case, and strictly speaking, the Devil of East Lupton, Vermont, was the Whatever-it-was which was in a leathery, hidelike garment or pressure-suit the morning Mr. Tedder ran away from the constable. And that Devil was destroyed by a rusty barbed wire which was strung between two trees on an abandoned farm. And it was killed long before so much as the existence of a Devil in those parts was suspected.

SCRIMSHAW

All hard-bitten SF fans are nostalgic: the good-old-days syndrome seems to be found in force wherever there is a gathering of them. Some stories are more successful than others in bringing back the very smell and feel of second-grade mechanical-pulp stock. This is one: is it really only twenty years ago that we were carving models out of chunks of 'Perspex'?

POP YOUNG was the one known man who could stand life on the surface of the Moon's far side, and therefore, he occupied the shack on the Big Crack's edge, above the mining colony there. Some people said that no normal man could do it, and mentioned the scar of a ghastly head-wound to explain his ability. One man partly guessed the secret, but only partly. His name was Sattell and he had reason not to talk. Pop Young alone knew the whole truth, and he kept his mouth shut, too. It wasn't anybody else's business.

The shack and the job he filled were located in the medieval notion of the physical appearance of hell. By day the environment was heat and torment. By night – lunar night, of course, and lunar day – it was frigidity and horror. Once in two weeks Earth-time a rocketship came around the horizon from Lunar City with stores for the colony deep underground. Pop received the stores and took care of them. He handed over the product of the mine, to be forwarded to Earth. The rocket went away again. Come nightfall Pop lowered the supplies down the long cable into the Big Crack to the colony far down inside, and freshened up the landing field marks with magnesium marking-powder if a rocket-blast had blurred them. That was fundamentally all he had to do. But without him the mine down in the Crack would have had to shut down.

The Crack, of course, was that gaping rocky fault which stretches nine hundred miles, jaggedly, over the side of the Moon that Earth never sees. There is one stretch where it is a yawning gulf a full half-mile wide and unguessably deep. Where Pop Young's shack stood it was only a hundred yards, but the colony was a full mile down, in one wall. There is nothing like it on Earth, of course. When it was first found, scientists descended into it to examine the exposed rock-strata and learn the history of the Moon before its craters were made. But they found more than history. They found the reason for the colony and the rocket landing field and the shack.

The reason for Pop was something else.

The shack stood a hundred feet from the Big Crack's edge. It looked like a dust-heap thirty feet high, and it was. The outside was surface moon-dust, piled over a tiny dome to be insulation against the cold of night and shadow and the furnace heat of day. Pop lived in it all alone, and in his spare time he worked industriously at recovering some missing portions of his life that Sattell had managed to take away from him.

He thought often of Sattell, down in the colony underground. There were galleries and tunnels and living-quarters down there. There were air-tight bulkheads for safety, and a hydroponic garden to keep the air fresh, and all sorts of things to make life possible for men under if not on the Moon.

But it wasn't fun, even underground. In the Moon's slight gravity, a man is really adjusted to existence when he has a well-developed case of agoraphobia. With such an aid, a man can get into a tiny, coffinlike cubbyhole, and feel solidity above and below and around him, and happily tell himself that it feels delicious. Sometimes it does.

But Sattell couldn't comfort himself so easily. He knew about Pop, up on the surface. He'd shipped out, whimpering, to the Moon to get far away from Pop, and Pop was just about a mile overhead and there was no way to get around him. It was difficult to get away from the mine, anyhow. It doesn't take too long for the low gravity to tear a man's nerves to shreds. He has to develop kinks in his head to survive. And those kinks—

The first men to leave the colony had to be knocked cold and shipped out unconscious. They'd been underground – and in low gravity – long enough to be utterly unable to face the idea of open spaces. Even now there were some who had to be carried, but there were some tougher ones who were able to walk to the rocketship if Pop put a tarpaulin over their heads so they didn't have to see the sky. In any case Pop was essential, either for carrying or guidance.

Sattell got the shakes when he thought of Pop, and Pop rather probably knew it. Of course, by the time he took the job tending the shack, he was pretty certain about Sattell. The facts spoke for themselves.

Pop had come back to consciousness in a hospital with a great wound in his head and no memory of anything that had happened before that moment. It was not that his identity was in question. When he was stronger, the doctors told him who he was, and as gently as possible what had happened to his wife and children. They'd been murdered after he was seemingly killed defending them. But he didn't remember a thing. Not then. It was something of a blessing.

But when he was physically recovered he set about trying to pick up the threads of the life he could no longer remember. He met Sattell quite by accident. Sattell looked familiar. Pop eagerly tried to ask him questions. And Sattell turned gray and frantically denied that he'd ever seen Pop before.

All of which happened back on Earth and a long time ago. It seemed to Pop that the sight of Sattell had brought back some vague and cloudy memories. They were not sharp, though, and he hunted up Sattell again to find out if he was right. And Sattell went into a panic when he returned.

Nowadays, by the Big Crack, Pop wasn't so insistent on seeing Sattell, but he was deeply concerned with the recovery of the memories that Sattell helped bring back. Pop was a highly conscientious man. He took good care of his job. There was a warning-bell in the shack, and when a rocketship from Lunar City got above the horizon and could send a tight beam, the gong clanged loudly, and Pop got into a vacuum-suit and went out the air lock. He usually reached the moondozer about the time the ship began to brake for landing, and he watched it come in.

He saw the silver needle in the sky fighting momentum above a line of jagged crater-walls. It slowed, and slowed, and curved down as it drew nearer. The pilot killed all forward motion just above the field and came steadily and smoothly down to land between the silvery triangles that marked the landing place.

Instantly the rockets cut off, drums of fuel and air and food came out of the cargo-hatch and Pop swept forward with the dozer. It was a miniature tractor with a gigantic scoop in front. He pushed a great mound of talc-fine dust before him to cover up the cargo. It was necessary. With freight costing what it did, fuel and air and food came frozen solid, in containers barely thicker than foil. While they stayed at space-shadow temperature, the foil would hold anything. And a cover of insulating moon-dust with vacuum between the grains kept even air frozen solid, though in sunlight.

At such times Pop hardly thought of Sattell. He knew he had plenty of time for that. He'd started to follow Sattell knowing what had happened to his wife and children, but it was hearsay only. He had no memory of them at all. But Sattell stirred the lost memories. At first Pop followed absorbedly from city to city, to recover the years that had been wiped out by an axe-blow. He did recover a good deal. When Sattell fled to another continent, Pop followed because he had some distinct memories of his wife – and the way he'd felt about her – and some fugitive mental images of his children. When Sattell frenziedly tried to deny knowledge of the murder in Tangier, Pop had come to remember both his children and some of the happiness of his married life.

Even when Sattell – whimpering – signed up for Lunar City, Pop tracked him. By that time he was quite sure that Sattell was the man who'd killed his family. If so, Sattell had profited by less than two days' pay for wiping out everything that Pop possessed. But Pop wanted it back. He couldn't prove Sattell's guilt. There was no evidence. In any case, he didn't really want Sattell to die. If he did, there'd be no way to recover more lost memories.

Sometimes, in the shack on the far side of the Moon, Pop Young had odd fancies about Sattell. There was the mine, for example. In each two Earth-weeks of working, the mine-colony nearly filled up a three-gallon cannister with greasy-seeming white crystals shaped like two pyramids base to base. The filled cannister would weigh a hundred pounds on Earth. Here it weighed eighteen. But on Earth its contents would be computed in carats, and a hundred pounds was worth millions. Yet here on the Moon Pop kept a waiting cannister on a shelf in his tiny dome, behind the air-apparatus. It rattled if he shook it, and it was worth no more than so many pebbles. But sometimes Pop wondered if Sattell ever thought of the value of the mine's production. If he would kill a woman and two children and think he'd killed a man for no more than a hundred dollars, what enormity would he commit for a three-gallon quantity of uncut diamonds?

But he did not dwell on such speculation. The sun rose very, very slowly in what by convention was called the east. It took nearly two hours to urge its disk above the horizon, and it burned terribly in emptiness for fourteen times twenty-four hours before sunset. Then there was night, and for three hundred and thirty-six consecutive hours there were only stars overhead and the sky was a hole so terrible that a man who looked up into it – what with the nagging sensation of one-sixth gravity – tended to lose all confidence in the stability of things. Most men immediately found it hysterically necessary to seize hold of something solid to keep from falling upward. But nothing felt solid. Everything fell, too. Wherefore most men tended to scream.

But not Pop. He'd come to the Moon in the first place because Sattell was here. Near Sattell, he found memories of times when he was a young man with a young wife who loved him extravagantly. Then pictures of his children came out of emptiness and grew sharp and clear. He found that he loved them very dearly. And when he was near Sattell he literally recovered them in the sense that he came to know new things about them and had new memories of them every day. He hadn't yet remembered the crime which lost them to him. Until he did – and the fact possessed a certain grisly humor – Pop didn't even hate Sattell. He simply wanted to be near him because it enabled him to recover new and vivid parts of his youth that had been lost.

Otherwise, he was wholly matter-of-fact – certainly so for the far side of the Moon. He was a rather fussy housekeeper. The shack above the Big Crack's rim was as tidy as any lighthouse or fur-trapper's cabin. He tended his air-apparatus with a fine precision. It was perfectly simple. In the shadow of the shack he had an unfailing source of extreme low temperature. Air from the shack flowed into a shadow-chilled pipe. Moisture condensed out of it here, and Co_2 froze solidly out of it there, and on beyond it collected as restless, transparent liquid air. At the same time, liquid air from another tank evaporated to maintain the proper air pressure in the shack. Every so often Pop tapped the pipe where the moisture froze, and lumps of water ice clattered out to be returned to the humidifier. Less often he took out the CO_2 snow, and measured it, and dumped an equivalent quantity of pale-blue liquid oxygen into the liquid air that had been purified by cold. The oxygen dissolved. Then the apparatus reversed itself and supplied fresh air from the now-enriched fluid, while the depleted other tank began to fill up with cold-purified liquid air.

Outside the shack, jagged stony pinnacles reared in the starlight, and craters complained of the bombardment from space that had made them. But, outside, nothing ever happened. Inside, it was quite different.

Working on his memories, one day Pop made a little sketch. It helped a great deal. He grew deeply interested. Writing-material was scarce, but he spent most of the time between two particular rocket-landings getting down on paper exactly how a child had looked while sleeping, some fifteen years before. He remembered with astonishment that the child had really looked exactly like that! Later he began a sketch of his partly-remembered wife. In time – he had plenty – it became a really truthful likeness.

The sun rose, and baked the abomination of desolation which was the moonscape. Pop Young meticulously touched up the glittering triangles which were landing guides for the Lunar City ships. They glittered from the thinnest conceivable layer of magnesium marking-powder. He checked over the moon-dozer. He tended the air apparatus. He did everything that his job and survival required. Ungrudgingly.

Then he made more sketches. The images to be drawn came back more clearly when he thought of Sattell, so by keeping Sattell in mind he recovered the memory of a chair that had been in his forgotten home. Then he drew his wife sitting in it, reading. It felt very good to see her again. And he speculated about whether Sattell ever thought of millions of dollars' worth of new-mined diamonds knocking about unguarded in the shack, and he suddenly recollected clearly the way one of his children had looked while playing with her doll. He made a quick sketch to keep from forgetting that.

There was no purpose in the sketching, save that he'd lost all his young manhood through a senseless crime. He wanted his youth back. He was recovering it bit by bit. The occupation made it absurdly easy to live on the surface of the far side of the Moon, whether anybody else could do it or not.

Sattell had no such device for adjusting to the lunar state of things. Living on the Moon was bad enough anyhow, then, but living one mile underground from Pop Young was much worse. Sattell clearly remembered the crime Pop Young hadn't yet recalled. He considered that Pop had made no overt attempt to revenge himself because he planned some retaliation so horrible and lingering that it was worth waiting for. He came to hate Pop with an insane ferocity. And fear. In his mind the need to escape became an obsession on top of the other psychotic states normal to a Moon-colonist.

But he was helpless. He couldn't leave. There was Pop. He couldn't kill Pop. He had no chance – and he was afraid. The one absurd, irrelevant thing he could do was write letters back to Earth. He did that. He wrote with the desperate, impassioned, frantic blend of persuasion and information and genius-like invention of a prisoner in a high-security prison, trying to induce someone to help him escape.

He had friends, of a sort, but for a long time his letters produced nothing. The Moon swung in vast circles about the Earth, and the Earth swung sedately about the Sun. The other planets danced their saraband. The rest of humanity went about its own affairs with fascinated attention. But then an event occurred which bore directly upon Pop Young and Sattell and Pop Young's missing years.

Somebody back on Earth promoted a luxury passenger-line of spaceships to ply between Earth and Moon. It looked like a perfect set-up. Three spacecraft capable of the journey came into being with attendant reams of publicity. They promised a thrill and a new distinction for the rich. Guided tours to Lunar! The most expensive and most thrilling trip in history! One hundred thousand dollars for a twelve-day cruise through space, with views of the Moon's far side and trips through Lunar City and a landing in Aristarchus, plus sound-tapes of the journey and fame hitherto reserved for honest explorers!

It didn't seem to have anything to do with Pop or with Sattell. But it did.

There were just two passenger tours. The first was fully booked. But the passengers who paid so highly, expected to be pleasantly thrilled and shielded from all reasons for alarm. And they couldn't be. Something happens when a self-centered and complacent individual unsuspectingly looks out of a spaceship port and sees the cosmos unshielded by mists or clouds or other aids to blindness against reality. It is shattering.

A millionaire cut his throat when he saw Earth dwindled to a mere blue-green ball in vastness. He could not endure his own smallness in the face of immensity. Not one passenger disembarked even for Lunar City. Most of them cowered in their chairs, hiding their eyes. They were the simple cases of hysteria. But the richest girl on Earth, who'd had five husbands and believed that nothing could move her – she went into catatonic withdrawal and neither saw nor heard nor moved. Two other passengers sobbed in improvised strait jackets. The first shipload started home. Fast.

The second luxury liner took off with only four passengers and turned back before reaching the Moon. Space-pilots could take the strain of space-flight because they had work to do. Workers for the lunar mines could make the trip under heavy sedation. But it was too early in the development of space-travel for pleasure-passengers. They weren't prepared for the more humbling facts of life.

Pop heard of the quaint commercial enterprise through the micro-tapes put off at the shack for the men down in the mine. Sattell probably learned of it the same way. Pop didn't even think of it again. It seemed to have nothing to do with him. But Sattell undoubtedly dealt with it fully in his desperate writings back to Earth.

Pop matter-of-factly tended the shack and the landing field and the stores for the Big Crack mine. Between-times he made more drawings in pursuit of his own private objective. Quite accidentally, he developed a certain talent professional artists might have approved. But he was not trying to communicate, but to discover. Drawing – especially with his mind on Sattell – he found fresh incidents popping up in his recollection. Times when he was happy. One day he remembered the puppy his children had owned and loved. He drew it painstakingly – and it was his again. Thereafter he could remember it any time he chose. He did actually recover a completely vanished past.

He envisioned a way to increase that recovery. But there was a marked shortage of artists' materials on the Moon. All freight had to be hauled from Earth, on a voyage equal to rather more than a thousand times around the equator of the Earth. Artists' supplies were not often included. Pop didn't even ask.

He began to explore the area outside the shack for possible material no one could think of sending from Earth. He collected stones of various sorts, but when warmed up in the shack they were useless. He found no strictly lunar material which would serve for modeling or carving portraits in the ground. He found minerals which could be pulverized and used as pigments, but nothing suitable for this new adventure in the recovery of lost youth. He even considered blasting, to aid his search. He could. Down in the mine, blasting was done by soaking carbon black – from CO_2 in liquid oxygen, and then firing it with a spark. It exploded splendidly. And its fumes were merely more CO_2 which an air-apparatus handled easily.

He didn't do any blasting. He didn't find any signs of the sort of mineral he required. Marble would have been perfect, but there is no marble on the Moon. Naturally! Yet Pop continued to search absorbedly for material with which to capture memory. Sattell still seemed necessary, but—

Early one lunar morning he was a good two miles from his shack when he saw rocket-fumes in the sky. It was most unlikely. He wasn't looking for anything of the sort, but out of the corner of his eye he observed that something moved. Which was impossible. He turned his head, and there were rocket-fumes coming over the horizon, not in the direction of Lunar City. Which was more impossible still.

He stared. A tiny silver rocket to the westward poured out monstrous masses of vapor. It decelerated swiftly. It curved downward. The rockets checked for an instant, and flamed again more violently, and checked once more. This was not an expert approach. It was a faulty one. Curving surfaceward in a sharply changing parabola, the pilot over-corrected and had to wait to gather down-speed, and then over-corrected again. It was an altogether clumsy landing. The ship was not even perfectly vertical when it settled not quite in the landing-area marked by silvery triangles. One of its tail-fins crumpled slightly. It tilted a little when fully landed.

Then nothing happened.

Pop made his way toward it in the skittering, skating gait one uses in one-sixth gravity. When he was within half a mile, an air-lock door opened in the ship's side. But nothing came out of the lock. No space-suited figure. No cargo came drifting down with the singular deliberation of falling objects on the Moon.

It was just barely past lunar sunrise on the far side of the Moon. Incredibly long and utterly black shadows stretched across the plain, and half the rocketship was dazzling white and half was blacker than blackness itself. The sun still hung low indeed in the black, star-speckled sky. Pop waded through the moondust, raising a trail of slowly settling powder. He knew only that the ship didn't come from Lunar City, but from Earth. He couldn't imagine why. He did not even wildly connect it with what – say – Sattell might have written with desperate plausibility about greasy-seeming white crystals out of the mine, knocking about Pop Young's shack in cannisters containing a hundred Earth-pounds weight of richness.

Pop reached the rocketship. He approached the big tail-fins. On one of them there were welded ladder-rungs going up to the opened air-lock door.

He climbed.

The air-lock was perfectly normal when he reached it. There was a glass port in the inner door, and he saw eyes looking through it at him. He pulled the outer door shut and felt the whining vibration of admitted air. His vacuum suit went slack about him. The inner door began to open, and Pop reached up and gave his helmet the practiced twisting jerk which removed it.

Then he blinked. There was a red-headed man in the opened door. He grinned savagely at Pop. He held a very nasty hand-weapon trained on Pop's middle.

'Don't come in!' he said mockingly. 'And I don't give a damn about how you are. This isn't social. It's business!'

Pop simply gaped. He couldn't quite take it in.

'This,' snapped the red-headed man abruptly, 'is a stickup!'

Pop's eyes went through the inner lock-door. He saw that the interior of the ship was stripped and bare. But a spiral stairway descended from some upper compartment. It had a handrail of pure, transparent, water-clear plastic. The walls were bare insulation, but that trace of luxury remained. Pop gazed at the plastic, fascinated.

The red-headed man leaned forward, snarling. He slashed Pop across the face with the barrel of his weapon. It drew blood. It was wanton, savage brutality.

'Pay attention!' snarled the red-headed man. 'A stickup, I

said! Get it? You go get that can of stuff from the mine! The diamonds! Bring them here! Understand?'

Pop said numbly: 'What the hell?'

The red-headed man hit him again. He was nerve-racked, and, therefore, he wanted to hurt.

'Move!' he rasped. 'I want the diamonds you've got for the ship from Lunar City! Bring 'em!' Pop licked blood from his lips and the man with the weapon raged at him. 'Then phone down to the mine! Tell Sattell I'm here and he can come on up! Tell him to bring any more diamonds they've dug up since the stuff you've got!'

He leaned forward. His face was only inches from Pop Young's. It was seamed and hard-bitten and nerve-racked. But any man would be quivering if he wasn't used to space or the feel of one-sixth gravity on the Moon. He panted:

'And get it straight! You try any tricks and we take off! We swing over your shack! The rocket-blast smashes it! We burn you down! Then we swing over the cable down to the mine and the rocket-flame melts it! You die and everybody in the mine besides! No tricks! We didn't come here for nothing!'

He twitched all over. Then he struck cruelly again at Pop Young's face. He seemed filled with fury, at least partly hysterical. It was the tension that space-travel – then, at its beginning – produced. It was meaningless savagery due to terror. But, of course, Pop was helpless to resent it. There were no weapons on the Moon and the mention of Sattell's name showed the uselessness of bluff. He'd pictured the complete set-up by the edge of the Big Crack. Pop could do nothing.

The red-headed man checked himself, panting. He drew back and slammed the inner lock-door. There was the sound of pumping.

Pop put his helmet back on and sealed it. The outer door opened. Outrushing air tugged at Pop. After a second or two he went out and climbed down the welded-on ladder-bars to the ground.

He headed back toward his shack. Somehow, the mention of Sattell had made his mind work better. It always did. He began painstakingly to put things together. The red-headed man knew the routine here in every detail. He knew Sattell. That part was simple. Sattell had planned his multi-million-dollar coup, as a man in prison might plan his break. The stripped interior of the ship identified it.

It was one of the unsuccessful luxury-liners sold for scrap. Or perhaps it was stolen for the journey here. Sattell's associates had had to steal or somehow get the fuel, and somehow find a pilot. But there were diamonds worth at least five million dollars waiting for them, and the whole job might not have called for more than two men – with Sattell as a third. According to the economics of crime, it was feasible. Anyhow it was being done.

Pop reached the dust-heap which was his shack and went in the air lock. Inside, he went to the vision-phone and called the mine-colony down in the Crack. He gave the message he'd been told to pass on. Sattell to come up, with what diamonds had been dug since the regular cannister was sent up for the Lunar City ship that would be due presently. Otherwise the ship on the landing strip would destroy shack and Pop and the colony together.

'I'd guess,' said Pop painstakingly, 'that Sattell figured it out. He's probably got some sort of gun to keep you from holding him down there. But he won't know his friends are here – not right this minute he won't.'

A shaking voice asked questions from the vision-phone.

'No,' said Pop, 'they'll do it anyhow. If we were able to tell about 'em, they'd be chased. But if I'm dead and the shack smashed and the cable burnt through, they'll be back on Earth long before a new cable's been got and let down to you. So they'll do all they can no matter what I do.' He added, 'I wouldn't tell Sattell a thing about it, if I were you. It'll save trouble. Just let him keep on waiting for this to happen. It'll save you trouble.'

Another shaky question.

'Me?' asked Pop. 'Oh, I'm going to raise what hell I can. There's some stuff in that ship I want.'

He switched off the phone. He went over to his air apparatus. He took down the cannister of diamonds which were worth five millions or more back on Earth. He found a bucket. He dumped the diamonds casually into it. They floated downward with great deliberation and surged from side to side like a liquid when they stopped. One-sixth gravity.

Pop regarded his drawings meditatively. A sketch of his wife as he now remembered her. It was very good to remember. A drawing of his two children, playing together. He looked forward to remembering much more about them. He grinned.

'That stair-rail,' he said in deep satisfaction. 'That'll do it!'

He tore bed linen from his bunk and worked on the emptied cannister. It was a double container with a thermware interior lining. Even on Earth newly-mined diamonds sometimes fly to pieces from internal stress. On the Moon, it was not desirable that diamonds be exposed to repeated violent changes of temperature. So a thermware-lined cannister kept them at mine-temperature once they were warmed to touchability.

Pop packed the cotton cloth in the container. He hurried a little, because the men in the rocket were shaky and might not practice patience. He took a small emergency-lamp from his spare spacesuit. He carefully cracked its bulb, exposing the filament within. He put the lamp on top of the cotton and sprinkled magnesium marking-powder over everything. Then he went to the air-apparatus and took out a flask of the liquid oxygen used to keep his breathing-air in balance. He poured the frigid, pale-blue stuff into the cotton. He saturated it.

All the inside of the shack was foggy when he finished. Then he pushed the cannister-top down. He breathed a sigh of relief when it was in place. He'd arranged for it to break a frozen-brittle switch as it descended. When it came off, the switch would light the lamp with its bare filament. There was powdered magnesium in contact with it and liquid oxygen all about.

He went out of the shack by the air lock. On the way, thinking about Sattell, he suddenly recovered a completely new memory. On their first wedding anniversary, so long ago, he and his wife had gone out to dinner to celebrate. He remembered how she looked: the almost-smug joy they shared that they would be together for always, with one complete year for proof.

Pop reflected hungrily that it was something else to be made permanent and inspected from time to time. But he wanted more than a drawing of this! He wanted to make the memory permanent and to extend it—

If it had not been for his vacuum suit and the cannister he carried, Pop would have rubbed his hands.

Tall, jagged crater-walls rose from the lunar plain. Monstrous, extended inky shadows stretched enormous distances, utterly black. The sun, like a glowing octopod, floated low at the edge of things and seemed to hate all creation.

Pop reached the rocket. He climbed the welded ladder-rungs to the air lock. He closed the door. Air whined. His suit sagged against his body. He took off his helmet.

When the red-headed man opened the inner door, the hand-weapon shook and trembled. Pop said calmly:

'Now I've got to go handle the hoist, if Sattell's coming up from the mine. If I don't do it, he don't come up.'

The red-headed man snarled. But his eyes were on the cannister whose contents should weigh a hundred pounds on Earth.

'Any tricks,' he rasped, 'and you know what happens!'

'Yeah,' said Pop.

He stolidly put his helmet back on. But his eyes went past the red-headed man to the stair that wound down, inside the ship, from some compartment above. The stair-rail was pure, clear, water-white plastic, not less than three inches thick. There was a lot of it!

The inner door closed. Pop opened the outer. Air rushed out. He climbed painstakingly down to the ground. He started back toward the shack.

There was the most luridly bright of all possible flashes. There was no sound, of course. But something flamed very brightly, and the ground thumped under Pop Young's vacuum boots. He turned.

The rocketship was still in the act of flying apart. It had been a splendid explosion. Of course cotton sheeting in liquid oxygen is not quite as good an explosive as carbon-black, which they used down in the mine. Even with magnesium powder to start the flame when a bare light-filament ignited it, the cannister-bomb hadn't equalled – say – T.N.T. But the ship had fuel on board for the trip back to Earth. And it blew, too. It would be minutes before all the fragments of the ship returned to the Moon's surface. On the Moon, things fall slowly.

Pop didn't wait. He searched hopefully. Once a mass of steel plating fell only yards from him, but it did not interrupt his search.

When he went into the shack, he grinned to himself. The call-light of the vision-phone flickered wildly. When he took off his helmet the bell clanged incessantly. He answered. A shaking voice from the mining-colony panted:

'We felt a shock! What happened? What do we do?'

'Don't do a thing,' advised Pop. 'It's all right. I blew up the ship and everything's all right. I wouldn't even mention it to Sattell if I were you.'

He grinned happily down at a section of plastic stair-rail he'd found not too far from where the ship exploded. When the man down in the mine cut off, Pop got out of his vacuum suit in a hurry. He placed the plastic zestfully on the table where he'd been restricted to drawing pictures of his wife and children in order to recover memories of them.

He began to plan, gloatingly, the thing he would carve out of a four-inch section of the plastic. When it was carved, he'd paint it. While he worked, he'd think of Sattell, because that was the way to get back the missing portions of his life – the parts Sattell had managed to get away from him. He'd get back more than ever, now!

He didn't wonder what he'd do if he ever remembered the crime Sattell had committed. He felt, somehow, that he wouldn't get that back until he'd recovered all the rest.

Gloating, it was amusing to remember what people used to call such art-works as he planned, when carved by other lonely men in other faraway places. They called those sculptures scrimshaw.

But they were a lot more than that!

IF YOU WAS A MOKLIN

Entertainment. For what more can you say of the last offering in this collection? After all, when you get right down to it that's what Leinster aimed for, first, foremost, and all the time. This item contains most of the ingredients that made Leinster's stories tick – a little science, a pinch of humor, a garnishing of feminine interest, a soupcon *of O'Henry.*

UP to the very last minute, I can't imagine that Moklin is going to be the first planet that humans get off of, moving fast, breathing hard, and sweating awful copious. There ain't any reason for it. Humans have been on Moklin for more than forty years, and nobody ever figures there is anything the least bit wrong until Brooks works it out. When he does, nobody can believe it. But it turns out bad. Plenty bad. But maybe things are working out all right now.

Maybe! I hope so.

At first, even after he's sent off long reports by six ships in a row, I don't see the picture beginning to turn sour. I don't get it until after the old *Palmyra* comes and squats down on the next to the last trip a Company ship is ever going to make to Moklin.

Up to that very morning everything is serene, and that morning I am sitting on the trading post porch, not doing a thing but sitting there and breathing happy. I'm looking at a Moklin kid. She's about the size of a human six-year-old and she is playing in a mud puddle while her folks are trading in the post. She is a cute kid – mighty human-looking. She has long whiskers like Old Man Bland, who's the first human to open a trading post and learn to talk to Moklins.

Moklins think a lot of Old Man Bland. They build him a big tomb, Moklin-style, when he dies, and there is more Moklin kids born with long whiskers than you can shake a stick at. And everything looks okay. *Everything!*

Sitting there on the porch, I hear a Moklin talking inside the trade room. Talking English just as good as anybody. He says to Deeth, our Moklin trade-clerk. 'But Deeth, I can buy this cheaper over at the other trading post! Why should I pay more here?'

Deeth says, in English too, 'I can't help that. That's the price here. You pay it or you don't. That's all.'

I just sit there breathing complacent, thinking how good things are. Here I'm Joe Brinkley, and me and Brooks are the Company on Moklin – only humans rate as Company employees and get pensions, of course – and I'm thinking sentimental about how much humaner Moklins are getting every day and how swell everything is.

The six-year-old kid gets up out of the mud puddle, and wrings out her whiskers – they are exactly like the ones on the picture of Old Man Bland in the trade room – and she goes trotting off down the road after her folks. She is mighty human-looking, that one.

The wild ones don't look near so human. Those that live in the forest are greenish, and have saucer eyes, and their noses can wiggle like an Earth rabbit. You wouldn't think they're the same breed as the trading post Moklins at all, but they are. They crossbreed with each other, only the kids look humaner than their parents and are mighty near the same skin color as Earthmen, which is plenty natural when you think about it, but nobody does. Not up to then.

I don't think about that then, or anything else. Not even about the reports Brooks keeps sweating over and sending off with every Company ship. I am just sitting there contented when I notice that Sally, the tree that shades the trading post porch, starts pulling up her roots. She gets them coiled careful and starts marching off. I see the other trees are moving off, too, clearing the landing field. They're waddling away to leave a free space, and they're pushing and shoving, trying to crowd each other, and the little ones sneak under the big ones and they all act peevish. Somehow they know a ship is coming in. That's what their walking off means, anyhow. But there ain't a ship due in for a month, yet.

They're clearing the landing field, though, so I start listening for a ship's drive, even if I don't believe it. At first I don't hear a thing. It must be ten minutes before I hear a thin whistle, and right after it the heavy drone that's the ground-repulsor units pushing against bedrock underground. Lucky they don't push on wet stuff, or a ship would sure mess up the local countryside!

I get off my chair and go out to look. Sure enough, the old *Palmyra* comes bulging down out of the sky, a month ahead of schedule, and the trees over at the edge of the field shove each other all round to make room. The ship drops, hangs anxious ten feet up, and then kind of sighs and lets down. Then there's Moklins running out of everywhere, waving cordial.

They sure do like humans, these Moklins! Humans are their idea of what people should be like! Moklins will wrestle the freight over to the trading post while others are climbing over everything that's waiting to go off, all set to pass it up to the ship and hoping to spot friends they've made in the crew. If they can get a human to go home with them and visit while the ship is down, they brag about it for weeks. And do they treat their guests swell!

They got fancy Moklin clothes for them to wear – soft, silky guest garments – and they got Moklin fruits and Moklin drinks – you ought to taste them! And when the humans have to go back to the ship at takeoff time, the Moklins bring them back with flower wreaths all over them.

Humans is tops on Moklin. And Moklins get humaner every day. There's Deeth, our clerk. You couldn't hardly tell him from human, anyways. He looks like a human named Casey that used to be at the trading post, and he's got a flock of brothers and sisters as human-looking as he is. You'd swear—

But this is the last time but one that a Earth ship is going to land on Moklin, though nobody knows it yet. Her passenger port opens up and Captain Haney gets out. The Moklins yell cheerful when they see him. He waves a hand and helps a human girl out. She has red hair and a sort of businesslike air about her. The Moklins wave and holler and grin. The girl looks at them funny, and Cap Haney explains something, but she sets her lips. Then the Moklins run out a freight-truck, and Haney and the girl get on it, and they come racing over to the post, the Moklins pushing and pulling them and making a big fuss of laughing and hollering – all so friendly, it would make anybody feel good inside. Moklins like humans! They admire them tremendous! They do everything they can think of to be human, and they're smart, but sometimes I get cold shivers when I think how close a thing it turns out to be.

Cap Haney steps off the freight-truck and helps the girl down. Her eyes are blazing. She is the maddest-looking female I ever see, but pretty as they make them, with that red hair and those blue eyes staring at me hostile.

'Hiya, Joe,' says Cap Haney. 'Where's Brooks?'

I tell him. Brooks is poking around in the mountains up back of the post. He is jumpy and worried and peevish, and he acts like he's trying to find something that ain't there, but he's bound he's going to find it regardless.

'Too bad he's not here,' says Haney. He turns to the girl. 'This is Joe Brinkley,' he says. 'He's Brooks' assistant. And, Joe, this is Inspector Caldwell – Miss Caldwell.'

'Inspector will do,' says the girl, curt. She looks at me accusing. 'I'm here to check into this matter of a competitive trading post on Moklin.'

'Oh,' I says. 'That's bad business. But it ain't cut into our trade much. In fact, I don't think it's cut our trade at all.'

'Get my baggage ashore, Captain,' says Inspector Caldwell, imperious. 'Then you can go about your business. I'll stay here until you stop on your return trip.'

I call, 'Hey, Deeth!' But he's right behind me. He looks respectful and admiring at the girl. You'd swear he's human! He's the spit and image of Casey, who used to be on Moklin until six years back.

'Yes, sir,' says Deeth. He says to the girl, 'Yes, ma'am. I'll show you your quarters, ma'am, and your baggage will get there right away. This way, ma'am.'

He leads her off, but he don't have to send for her baggage. A pack of Moklins come along, dragging it, hopeful of having her say 'Thank you' to them for it. There hasn't ever been a human woman on Moklin before, and they are all excited. I bet if there had been women around before, there'd have been hell loose before, too. But now the Moklins just hang around, admiring.

There are kids with whiskers like Old Man Bland, and other kids with mustaches – male and female both – and all that sort of stuff. I'm pointing out to Cap Haney some kids that bear a remarkable resemblance to him and he's saying, 'Well, what do you know!' when Inspector Caldwell comes back.

'What are you waiting for, Captain?' she asks, frosty.

'The ship usually grounds a few hours,' I explain. 'These Moklins are such friendly critters, we figure it makes good will for the trading post for the crew to be friendly with 'em.'

'I doubt,' says Inspector Caldwell, her voice dripping icicles, 'that I shall advise that that custom be continued.'

Cap Haney shrugs his shoulders and goes off, so I know Inspector Caldwell is high up in the Company. She ain't old, maybe in her middle twenties, I'd say, but the Caldwell family practically owns the Company, and all the nephews and cousins and so on get put into a special school so they can go to work in the family firm. They get taught pretty good, and most of them really rate the good jobs they get. Anyhow, there's plenty of good jobs. The Company runs twenty or thirty solar systems and it's run pretty tight. Being a Caldwell means you get breaks, but you got to live up to them.

Cap Haney almost has to fight his way through the Moklins who want to give him flowers and fruits and such. Moklins are sure crazy about humans! He gets to the entry port and goes in, and the door closes and the Moklins pull back. Then the *Palmyra* booms. The ground-repulsor unit is on. She heaves up, like she is grunting, and goes bulging up into the air, and the humming gets deeper and deeper, and fainter and fainter – and suddenly there's a keen whistling and she's gone. It's all very normal. Nobody would guess that this is the last time but one a Earth ship will ever lift off Moklin!

Inspector Caldwell taps her foot, icy. 'When will you send for Mr. Brooks?' she demands.

'Right away,' I says to her. 'Deeth–'

'I sent a runner for him, ma'am,' says Deeth. 'If he was in hearing of the ship's landing, he may be on the way here now.'

He bows and goes in the trade room. There are Moklins that came to see the ship land, and now have tramped over to do some trading. Inspector Caldwell jumps.

'Wh-what's that?' she asks, tense.

The trees that crowded off the field to make room for the *Palmyra* are waddling back. I realize for the first time that it might look funny to somebody just landed on Moklin. They are regular-looking trees, in a way. They got bark and branches and so on. Only they can put their roots down into holes they make in the ground, and that's the way they stay, mostly, but they can move. Wild ones, when there's a water shortage or they get too crowded or mad with each other, they pull up their roots and go waddling around looking for a better place to take root in.

The trees on our landing field have learned that every so often a ship is going to land and they've got to make room for it. But now the ship is gone, and they're lurching back to their places. The younger ones are waddling faster than the big ones, though, and taking the best places, and the old grunting trees are waving their branches indignant and puffing after them mad as hell.

I explain what is happening. Inspector Caldwell just stares. Then Sally comes lumbering up. I got a friendly feeling for Sally. She's pretty old – her trunk is all of three feet thick – but she always puts out a branch to shade my window in the morning, and I never let any other tree take her place. She comes groaning up, and uncoils her roots, and sticks them down one by one into the holes she'd left, and sort of scrunches into place and looks peaceful.

'Aren't they – dangerous?' asks Inspector Caldwell, pretty uneasy.

'Not a bit,' I says. 'Things can change on Moklin. They don't have to fight. Things fight in other places because they can't change and they get crowded, and that's the only way they can meet competition. But there's a special kind of evolution on Moklin. Cooperative, you might call it. It's a nice place to live.

Only thing is everything matures so fast. Four years and a Moklin is grown up, for instance.'

She sniffs. 'What about that other trading post?' she says, sharp. 'Who's back of it? The Company is supposed to have exclusive trading rights here. Who's trespassing?'

'Brooks is trying to find out,' I says. 'They got a good complete line of trade goods, but the Moklins always say the humans running the place have gone off somewhere, hunting and such. We ain't seen any of them.'

'No?' says the girl, short. '*I'll* see them! We can't have competition in our exclusive territory! The rest of Mr. Brooks' reports—' She stops. Then she says, 'That clerk of yours reminds me of someone I know.'

'He's a Moklin,' I explain, 'but he looks like a Company man named Casey. Casey's Area Director over on Khatim Two now, but he used to be here, and Deeth is the spit and image of him.'

'Outrageous!' says Inspector Caldwell, looking disgusted.

There's a couple of trees pushing hard at each other. They are fighting, tree-fashion, for a specially good place. And there's others waddling around, mad as hell, because somebody else beat them to the spots they liked. I watch them. Then I grin, because a couple of young trees duck under the fighting big ones and set their roots down in the place the big trees was fighting over.

'I don't like your attitude!' says Inspector Caldwell, furious.

She goes stamping into the post, leaving me puzzled. What's wrong with me smiling at those kid trees getting the best of their betters?

That afternoon Brooks comes back, marching ahead of a pack of woods-Moklins with greenish skins and saucer eyes that've been guiding him around. He's a good-looking kind of fellow, Brooks is, with a good build and a solid jaw.

When he comes out of the woods on the landing field – the trees are all settled down by then – he's striding impatient and loose-jointed. With the woods-Moklins trailing him, he looks plenty dramatic, like a visi-reel picture of a explorer on some unknown planet, coming back from the dark and perilous forests, followed by the strange natives who do not yet know whether this visitor from outer space is a god or what. You know the stuff.

I see Inspector Caldwell take a good look at him, and I see her eyes widen. She looks like he is a shock, and not a painful one.

He blinks when he sees her. He grunts, 'What's this? A she-Moklin?'

Inspector Caldwell draws herself up to her full five-foot-three. She bristles.

I say quick, 'This here is Inspector Caldwell that the *Palmyra* dumped off here today. Uh – Inspector, this is Brooks, the Head Trader.'

They shake hands. He looks at her and says, 'I'd lost hope my reports would ever get any attention paid to them. You've come to check my report that the trading post on Moklin has to be abandoned?'

'I have not!' says Inspector Caldwell, sharp. 'That's absurd! This planet has great potentialities, this post is profitable and the natives are friendly, and the trade should continue to increase. The Board is even considering the introduction of special crops.'

That strikes me as a bright idea. I'd like to see what would happen if Moklins started cultivating new kinds of plants! It would be a thing to watch – with regular Moklin plants seeing strangers getting good growing places and special attention! I can't even guess what'll happen, but I want to watch!

'What I want to ask right off,' says Inspector Caldwell, fierce, 'is why you have allowed a competitive trading post to be established, why you did not report it sooner, and why you haven't identified the company back of it?'

Brooks stares at her. He gets mad.

'Hell!' he says. 'My reports cover all that! Haven't you read them?'

'Of course not,' says Inspector Caldwell. 'I was given an outline of the situation here and told to investigate and correct it.'

'Oh!' says Brooks. 'That's it!'

Then he looks like he's swallowing naughty words. It is funny to see them glare at each other, both of them looking like they are seeing something that interests them plenty, but throwing off angry sparks just the same.

'If you'll show me samples of their trade goods,' says Inspector Caldwell, arrogant, 'and I hope you can do *that* much, I'll identify the trading company handling them!'

He grins at her without amusement and leads the way to the inside of the trading post. We bring out the stuff we've had some of our Moklins go over and buy for us. Brooks dumps the goods on a table and stands back to see what she'll make of them, grinning with the same lack of mirth. She picks up a visireel projector.

'Hmm,' she says, scornful. 'Not very good quality. It's . . .' Then she stops. She picks up a forest knife. 'This,' she says, 'is a product of—' Then she stops again. She picks up some cloth and fingers it. She really steams. 'I see!' she says, angry. 'Because we have been on this planet so long and the Moklins are used to our goods, the people of the other trading post *duplicate* them! Do they cut prices?'

'Fifty per cent,' says Brooks.

I chime in, 'But we ain't lost much trade. Lots of Moklins still trade with us, out of friendship. Friendly folks, these Moklins.'

Just then Deeth comes in, looking just like Casey that used to be here on Moklin. He grins at me.

'A girl just brought you a compliment,' he lets me know.

'Shucks!' I says, embarrassed and pleased. 'Send her in and get a present for her.'

Deeth goes out. Inspector Caldwell hasn't noticed. She's seething over that other trading company copying our trade goods and underselling us on a planet we're supposed to have exclusive. Brooks looks at her grim.

'I shall look over their post,' she announces, fierce, 'and if they want a trade war, they'll get one! We can cut prices if we need to – we have all the resources of the Company behind us!'

Brooks seems to be steaming on his own, maybe because she

hasn't read his reports. But just then a Moklin girl comes in. Not bad-looking, either. You can see she is a Moklin – she ain't as convincing human as Deeth is, say – but she looks pretty human, at that. She giggles at me.

'Compliment,' she says, and shows me what she's carrying.

I look. It's a Moklin kid, a boy, just about brand-new. And it has my shape ears, and its nose looks like somebody had stepped on it – my nose is that way – and it looks like a very small-sized working model of me. I chuck it under the chin and say, 'Kitchy-coo!' It gurgles at me.

'What's your name?' I ask the girl.

She tells me. I don't remember it, and I don't remember ever seeing her before, but she's paid me a compliment, all right – Moklin-style.

'Mighty nice,' I say. 'Cute as all get-out. I hope he grows up to have more sense than I got, though.' Then Deeth comes in with a armload of trade stuff like Old Man Bland gave to the first Moklin kid that was born with long whiskers like his, and I say, 'Thanks for the compliment. I am greatly honored.'

She takes the stuff and giggles again, and goes out. The kid beams at me over her shoulder and waves its fist. Mighty humanlike. A right cute kid, anyway you look at it.

Then I hear a noise. Inspector Caldwell is regarding me with loathing in her eyes.

'Did you say they were friendly creatures?' she asks, bitter. 'I think affectionate would be a better word!' Her voice shakes. 'You are going to be transferred out of here the instant the *Palmyra* gets back!'

'What's the matter?' I ask, surprised. 'She paid me a compliment and I gave her a present. It's a custom. She's satisfied. I never see her before that I remember.'

'You *don't*?' she says. 'The – the *callousness*! You're revolting!'

Brooks begins to sputter, then he snickers, and all of a sudden he's howling with laughter. He is laughing at Inspector Caldwell. Then I get it, and I snort. Then I hoot and holler. It gets funnier when she gets madder still. She near blows up from being mad!

We must look crazy, the two of us there in the post, just hollering with laughter while she gets furiouser and furiouser. Finally I have to lay down on the floor to laugh more comfortable. You see, she doesn't get a bit of what I've told her about there being a special kind of evolution on Moklin. The more disgusted and furious she looks at me, the harder I have to laugh. I can't help it.

When we set out for the other trading post next day, the atmosphere ain't what you'd call exactly cordial. There is just the Inspector and me, with Deeth and a couple of other Moklins for the look of things. She has on a green forest suit, and with her red hair she sure looks good! But she looks at me cold when Brooks says I'll take her over to the other post, and she doesn't say a word the first mile or two.

We trudge on, and presently Deeth and the others get ahead so they can't hear what she says. And she remarks indignant, 'I must say Mr. Brooks isn't very cooperative. Why didn't he come with me? Is he afraid of the men at the other post?'

'Not him,' I says. 'He's a good guy. But you got authority over him and you ain't read his reports.'

'If I have authority,' she says, sharp, 'I assure you it's because I'm competent!'

'I don't doubt it,' I says. 'If you wasn't cute, he wouldn't care. But a man don't want a good-looking girl giving him orders. He wants to give them to her. A homely woman, it don't matter.'

She tosses her head, but it don't displease her. Then she says. 'What's in the reports that I should have read?'

'I don't know,' I admit. 'But he's been sweating over them. It makes him mad that nobody bothered to read 'em.'

'Maybe,' she guesses, 'it was what I need to know about this other trading post. What do you know about it, Mr. Brinkley?'

I tell her what Deeth has told Brooks. Brooks found out about it because one day some Moklins come in to trade and ask friendly why we charge so much for this and that. Deeth told them we'd always charged that, and they say the other trading post sells things cheaper, and Deeth says what trading post? So they up and tell him there's another post that sells the same kind of things we do, only cheaper. But that's all they'll say.

So Brooks tells Deeth to find out, and he scouts around and comes back. There is another trading post only fifteen miles away, and it is selling stuff just like ours. And it charges only half price. Deeth didn't see the men – just the Moklin clerks. We ain't been able to see the men either.

'Why haven't you seen the men?'

'Every time Brooks or me go over,' I explain, 'the Moklins they got working for them say the other men are off somewhere. Maybe they're starting some more posts. We wrote 'em a note, asking what the hell they mean, but they never answered it. Of course, we ain't seen their books or their living quarters—'

'You could find out plenty by a glimpse at their books!' she snaps. 'Why haven't you just marched in and made the Moklins show you what you want to know, since the men were away?'

'Because,' I says, patient, 'Moklins imitate humans. If we start trouble, they'll start it too. We can't set a example of rough stuff like burglary, mayhem, breaking and entering, manslaughter, or bigamy, or those Moklins will do just like us.'

'Bigamy!' She grabs on that sardonic. 'If you're trying to make me think you've got enough moral sense—'

I get a little mad. Brooks and me, we've explained to her, careful, how it is admiration *and* the way evolution works on Moklin that makes Moklin kids get born with long whiskers and that the compliment the Moklin girl has paid me is just exactly that. But she hasn't listened to a word.

'Miss Caldwell,' I says, 'Brooks and me told you the facts. We tried to tell them delicate, to spare your feelings. Now if you'll try to spare mine, I'll thank you.'

'If you mean your finer feelings,' she says, sarcastic, 'I'll spare them as soon as I find some!'

So I shut up. There's no use trying to argue with a woman. We tramp on through the forest without a word. Presently we come on a nest-bush. It's a pretty big one. There are a couple dozen nests on it, from the little-bitty bud ones no bigger than your fist, to the big ripe ones lined with soft stuff that have busted open and have got cacklebirds housekeeping in them now.

There are two cacklebirds sitting on a branch by the nest that is big enough to open up and have eggs laid in it, only it ain't. The cacklebirds are making noises like they are cussing it and telling it to hurry up and open, because they are in a hurry.

'That's a nest-bush,' I says. 'It grows nests for the cacklebirds. The birds – uh – fertilize the ground around it. They're sloppy feeders and drop a lot of stuff that rots and is fertilizer too. The nest-bush and the cacklebirds kind of cooperate. That's the way evolution works on Moklin, like Brooks and me told you.'

She tosses that red head of hers and stamps on, not saying a word. So we get to the other trading post. And there she gets one of these slow-burning, long-lasting mads on that fill a guy like me with awe.

There's only Moklins at the other trading post, as usual. They say the humans are off somewhere. They look at her admiring and polite. They show her their stock. It is practically identical with ours – only they admit that they've sold out of some items because their prices are low. They act most respectful and pleased to see her.

But she don't learn a thing about where their stuff comes from or what company is horning in on Moklin trade. And she looks at their head clerk and she burns and burns.

When we get back, Brooks is sweating over memorandums he has made, getting another report ready for the next Company ship. Inspector Caldwell marches into the trade room and gives orders in a controlled, venomous voice. Then she marches right in on Brooks.

'I have just ordered the Moklin sales force to cut the price on all items on sale by seventy-five per cent,' she says, her voice trembling a little with fury. 'I have also ordered the credit given for Moklin trade goods to be doubled. They want a trade war? They'll get it!'

She is a lot madder than business would account for. Brooks

says, tired, 'I'd like to show you some facts. I've been over every inch of territory in thirty miles, looking for a place where a ship could land for that other post. There isn't any: Does that mean anything to you?'

'The post is there, isn't it?' she says. 'And they have trade goods, haven't they? And we have exclusive trading rights on Moklin, haven't we? That's enough for me. Our job is to drive them out of business!'

But she is a lot madder than business would account for. Brooks says, very weary, 'There's nearly a whole planet where they could have put another trading post. They could have set up shop on the other hemisphere and charged any price they pleased. But they set up shop right next to us? Does that make sense?'

'Setting up close,' she says, 'would furnish them with customers already used to human trade goods. And it furnished them with Moklins trained to be interpreters and clerks! And—' Then it come out, what she's raging, boiling, steaming, burning up about. 'And,' she says, furious, 'it furnished them with a Moklin head-clerk who is a very handsome young man, Mr. Brooks! He not only resembles you in every feature, but he even has a good many of your mannerisms. You should be very proud!'

With this she slams out of the room. Brooks blinks.

'She won't believe anything,' he says, sour, 'except only that man is vile. Is that true about a Moklin who looks like me?'

I nod.

'Funny his folks never showed him to me for a compliment-present!' Then he stares at me, hard. 'How good is the likeness?'

'If he is wearing your clothes,' I tell him, truthful, 'I'd swear he is you.'

Then Brooks – slow, very slow – turns white. 'Remember the time you went off with Deeth and his folks hunting? That was the time a Moklin got killed. You were wearing guest garments weren't you?'

I feel queer inside, but I nod. Guest garments, for Moklins, are like the best bedroom and the drumstick of the chicken among humans. And a Moklin hunting party is something. They go hunting *garlikthos,* which you might as well call dragons, because they've got scales and they fly and they are tough babies.

The way to hunt them is you take along some cacklebirds that ain't nesting – they are no good for anything while they're honeymooning – and the cacklebirds go flapping around until a *garlikthos* comes after them, and then they go jet-streaking to where the hunters are, cackling a blue streak to say, 'Here I come, boys! Hold everything until I get past!' Then the *garlikthos* dives after them and the hunters get it as it dives.

You give the cacklebirds its innards, and they sit around and eat, cackling to each other, zestful, like they're bragging about the other times they done the same thing, only better.

'You were wearing guest garments?' repeats Brooks, grim.

I feel very queer inside, but I nod again. Moklin guest garments are mighty easy on the skin and feel mighty good. They ain't exactly practical hunting clothes, but the Moklins feel bad if a human that's their guest don't wear them. And of course he has to shed his human clothes to wear them.

'What's the idea?' I want to know. But I feel pretty unhappy inside.

'You didn't come back for one day, in the middle of the hunt, after tobacco and a bath?'

'No,' I says, beginning to get rattled. 'We were way over at the Thunlib Hills. We buried the dead Moklin over there and had a hell of a time building a tomb over him. Why?'

'During that week,' says Brooks, grim, 'and while you were off wearing Moklin guest garments, somebody came back wearing your clothes – and got some tobacco and passed the time of day and went off again. Joe, just like there's a Moklin you say could pass for me, there's one that could pass for you. In fact, he did. Nobody suspected either.'

I get panicky. 'But what'd he do that for?' I want to know. 'He didn't steal anything! Would he have done it just to brag to the other Moklins that he fooled you?'

'He might,' says Brooks, 'have been checking to see if he could fool me. Or Captain Haney of the *Palmyra.* Or—'

He looks at me. I feel myself going numb. This can mean one hell of a mess!

'I haven't told you before,' says Brooks, 'but I've been guessing at something like this. Moklins like to be human, and they get human kids – kids that look human, anyway. Maybe they can want to be smart like humans, and they are.' He tries to grin, and can't. 'That rival trading post looked fishy to me right at the start. They're practicing with that. It shouldn't be there at all, but it is. You see?'

I feel weak and sick all over. This is a dangerous sort of thing! But I say quick, 'If you mean they got Moklins that could pass for you and me, and they're figuring to bump us off and take our places – I don't believe that! Moklins *like* humans! They wouldn't harm humans for *anything*!'

Brooks don't pay any attention. He says, harsh, 'I've been trying to persuade the Company that we've got to get out of here, fast! And they send this Inspector Caldwell who's not only female, but a redhead to boot! All they think about is a competitive trading post! And all she sees is that we're a bunch of lascivious scoundrels, and since she's a woman there's nothing that'll convince her otherwise!'

Then something hits me. It looks hopeful.

'She's the first human woman to land on Moklin. And she has got red hair. It's the first red hair the Moklins ever saw. Have we got time?'

He figures. Then he says, 'With luck, it ought to turn up! You've hit it!' And then his expression sort of softens. 'If that happens – poor kid, she's going to take it hard! Women hate to be wrong. Especially redheads! But that might be the saving of – of humanity, when you think of it.'

I blink at him. He goes on, fierce, 'Look, *I'm* no Moklin! You know that. But if there's a Moklin that looks enough like me to take my place . . . You see? We got to think of Inspector Caldwell, anyhow. If you ever see me cross my fingers, you wiggle your little finger. Then I know it's you. And the other way about. Get it? You swear you'll watch over Inspector Caldwell?'

'Sure!' I say. 'Of course!'

I wiggle my little finger. He crosses his. It's a signal nobody but us two would know. I feel a lot better.

Brooks goes off next morning, grim, to visit the other trading post and see the Moklin that looks so much like him. Inspector Caldwell goes along, fierce, and I'm guessing it's to see the fireworks when Brooks sees his Moklin double that she thinks is more than a coincidence. Which she is right, only not in the way she thinks.

Before they go, Brooks crosses his fingers and looks at me significant. I wiggle my little finger back at him. They go off.

I sit down in the shade of Sally and try to think things out. I am all churned up inside, and scared as hell. It's near two weeks to landing time, when the old *Palmyra* ought to come bulging down out of the sky with a load of new trade goods. I think wistful about how swell everything has been on Moklin up to now, and how Moklins admire humans, and how friendly everything has been, and how it's a great compliment for Moklins to want to be like humans and to get like them, and how no Moklin would ever dream of hurting a human and how they imitate humans joyous and reverent and happy. Nice people, Moklins. But—

The end of things is in sight. Liking humans has made Moklins smart, but now there's been a slip-up. Moklins will do anything to produce kids that look like humans. That's a compliment. But no human ever sees a Moklin that's four or five years old and all grown up and looks so much like him that nobody can tell them apart. That ain't scheming. It's just that Moklins like humans, but they're scared the humans might not like to see themselves in a sort of Moklin mirror. So if they did that at all, they'd maybe keep it a secret, like children keep secrets from grownups.

Moklins are a lot like kids. You can't help liking them. But a human can get plenty panicky if he thinks what would happen if Moklins get to passing for humans among humans, and want their kids to have top-grade brains, and top-grade talents, and so on . . .

I sweat, sitting there. I can see the whole picture. Brooks is worrying about Moklins loose among humans, outsmarting them as their kids grow up, being the big politicians, the bosses, the planetary pioneers, the prettiest girls and the handsomest guys in the Galaxy – everything humans want to be themselves. Just thinking about it is enough to make any human feel like he's going nuts. But Brooks is also worrying about Inspector Caldwell, who is five foot three and red-headed and cute as a bug's ear and riding for a bad fall.

They come back from the trip to the other trading post. Inspector Caldwell is baffled and mad. Brooks is sweating and scared. He slips me the signal and I wiggle my little finger back at him, just so I'll know he didn't get substituted for without Inspector Caldwell knowing it, and so he knows nothing happened to me while he was gone. They didn't see the Moklin that looks like Brooks. They didn't get a bit of information we didn't have before – which is just about none at all.

Things go on. Brooks and me are sweating it out until the *Palmyra* lets down out of the sky again, meanwhile praying for Inspector Caldwell to get her ears pinned back so proper steps can be taken, and every morning he crosses his fingers at me, and I wiggle my little finger back at him . . . And he watches over Inspector Caldwell tender.

The other trading post goes on placid. They sell their stuff at half the price we sell ours for. So, on Inspector Caldwell's orders, we cut ours again to half what they sell theirs for. So they sell theirs for half what we sell ours for, so we sell ours for half what they sell theirs for. And so on. Meanwhile we sweat.

Three days before the *Palmyra* is due, our goods are marked at just exactly one per cent of what they was marked a month before, and the other trading post is selling them at half that. It looks like we are going to have to pay a bonus to Moklins to take goods away for us to compete with the other trading post.

Otherwise, everything looks normal on the surface. Moklins hang around as usual, friendly and admiring. They'll hang around a couple of days just to get a look at Inspector Caldwell, and they regard her respectful.

Brooks looks grim. He is head over heels crazy about her now and she knows it, and she rides him hard. She snaps at him, and he answers her patient and gentle – because he knows that when what he hopes is going to happen, she is going to need him to comfort her. She has about wiped out our stock, throwing bargain sales. Our shelves are almost bare. But the other trading post still has plenty of stock.

'Mr. Brooks,' says Inspector Caldwell, bitter, at breakfast, 'we'll have to take most of the *Palmyra*'s cargo to fill up our inventory.'

'Maybe,' he says, tender, 'and maybe not.'

'But we've got to drive that other post out of business!' she says, desperate. Then she breaks down. 'This – this is my first independent assignment. I've got to handle it successfully!'

He hesitates. But just then Deeth comes in. He beams friendly at Inspector Caldwell.

'A compliment for you, ma'am. Three of them.'

She goggles at him. Brooks says, gentle, 'It's all right. Deeth, show them in and get some presents.'

Inspector Caldwell splutters incredulous, 'But – but—'

'Don't be angry,' says Brooks. 'They mean it as a compliment. It is, actually, you know.'

Three Moklin girls come in, giggling. They are not bad-looking at all. They look as human as Deeth, but one of them has a long, droopy mustache like a mate of the *Palmyra* – that's because they hadn't even seen a human woman before Inspector Caldwell come along. They sure have admired her, though! And Moklin kids get born fast. Very fast.

They show her what they are holding so proud and happy in their arms. They have got three little Moklin kids, one apiece. And every one of them has red hair, just like Inspector Caldwell, and every one of them is a girl that is the spit and image of her. You would swear they are human babies, and you'd swear they are hers. But of course they ain't. They make kid noises and wave their little fists.

Inspector Caldwell is just plain paralyzed. She stares at them, and goes red as fire and white as chalk, and she is speechless. So Brooks has to do the honors. He admires the kids extravagant, and the Moklin girls giggle, and take the compliment presents Deeth brings in, and they go out happy.

When the door closes, Inspector Caldwell wilts.

'Oh-h!' she wails. 'It's true! You didn't – you haven't – they can make their babies look like anybody they want!'

Brooks puts his arms around her and she begins to cry against his shoulder. He pats her and says, 'They've got a queer sort of evolution on Moklin, darling. Babies here inherit desired characteristics. Not *acquired* characteristics, but *desired* ones! And what could be more desirable than you?'

I am blinking at them. He says to me, cold, 'Will you kindly get the hell out of here and stay out?'

I come to. I says. 'Just one precaution.'

I wiggle my little finger. He crosses his fingers at me.

'Then,' I says, 'since there's no chance of a mistake, I'll leave you two together.'

And I do.

The *Palmyra* booms down out of the sky two days later. We are all packed up. Inspector Caldwell is shaky, on the porch of the post, when Moklins come hollering and waving friendly over from the landing field pulling a freight-truck with Cap Haney on it. I see the other festive groups around members of the crew that – this being a scheduled stop – have been given ship-leave for a couple hours to visit their Moklin friends.

'I've got the usual cargo—' begins Cap Haney.

'Don't discharge it,' says Inspector Caldwell, firm. 'We are abandoning this post. I have authority and Mr. Brooks has convinced me of the necessity for it. Please get our baggage to the ship.'

He gapes at her.'The Company don't like to give in to competition—'

'There isn't any competition,' says Inspector Caldwell. She gulps. 'Darling, you tell him,' she says to Brooks.

He says, lucid, 'She's right, Captain. The other trading post is purely a Moklin enterprise. They like to do everything that humans do. Since humans were running a trading post, they opened one too. They bought goods from us and pretended to sell them at half price, and we cut our prices, and they bought more goods from us and pretended to sell at half the new prices. . . . Some Moklin or other must've thought it would be nice to be a smart businessman, so his kids would be smart businessmen. Too smart! We close up this post before Moklins think of other things . . .'

He means, of course, that if Moklins get loose from their home planet and pass as humans, their kids can maybe take over human civilization. Human nature couldn't take that! But it is something to be passed on to the high brass, and not told around general.

'Better sound the emergency recall signal,' says Inspector Caldwell, brisk.

We go over to the ship and the *Palmyra* lets go that wailing siren that'll carry twenty miles. Any crew member in hearing is going to beat it back to the ship full-speed. They come running from every which way, where they been visiting their Moklin friends. And then, all of a sudden, here comes a fellow wearing Moklin guest garments, yelling, 'Hey! Wait! I ain't got my clothes—'

And then there is what you might call a dead silence. Because lined up for checkoff is another guy that comes running at the recall signal, and he is wearing ship's clothes, and you can see that him and the guy in Moklin guest garments are just exactly alike. Twins. Identical. The spit and image of each other. And it is for sure that one of them is a Moklin. But which?

Cap Haney's eyes start to pop out of his head. But then the guy in *Palmyra* uniform grins and says, 'Okay, I'm a Moklin. But us Moklins like humans so much, I thought it would be nice to make a trip to earth and see more humans. My parents planned it five years ago, made me look like this wonderful human, and hid me for this moment. But we would not want to make any difficulties for humans, so I have confessed and I will leave the ship.'

He takes it as a joke on him. He talks English as good as anybody. I don't know how anybody could tell which was the human guy and which one the Moklin, but this Moklin grins and steps down, and the other Moklins admire him enormous for passing even a few minutes as human among humans.

We get away from there so fast, he is allowed to keep the human uniform.

Moklin is the first planet that humans ever get off of, moving fast, breathing hard, and sweating copious. It's one of those things that humans just can't take. Not that there's anything wrong with Moklins. They're swell folks. They like humans. But humans just can't take the idea of Moklins passing for human and being all the things humans want to be themselves. I think it's really a false alarm. I'll find out pretty soon.

Inspector Caldwell and Brooks get married, and they go off to a post on Briarius Four – a swell place for a honeymoon if there ever was one – and I guess they are living happy ever after. Me, I go to the new job the Company assigns me – telling me stern not to talk about Moklin, which I don't – and the Space Patrol orders no human ship to land on Moklin for any reason.

But I've been saving money and worrying. I keep thinking of those three Moklin kids that Inspector Caldwell knows she ain't the father of. I worry about those kids. I hope nothing's happened to them. Moklin kids grow up fast, like I told you. They'll be just about grown now.

I'll tell you. I've bought me a little private spacecruiser, small but good. I'm shoving off for Moklin next week. If one of those three ain't married, I'm going to marry her, Moklin-style, and bring her out to a human colony planet. We'll have some kids. I know just what I want my kids to be like. They'll have plenty of brains – *top-level brains* – and the girls will be *real* good-looking!

But besides that, I've got to bring some other Moklins out and start them passing for human, too. Because my kids are going to need other Moklins to marry, ain't they? It's not that I don't like humans. I do! If the fellow I look like – Joe Brinkley – hadn't got killed accidental on that hunting trip with Deeth, I never would have thought of taking his place and being Joe

Brinkley. But you can't blame me for wanting to live among humans.

Wouldn't you, if you was a Moklin?

MURRAY LEINSTER

THE END

VAR THE STICK BY PIERS ANTHONY

VAR THE STICK is the second book in the trilogy.

Sol controlled the mountain and Sos the Empire. Two worlds so completely different from each other that they could not exist together on the same planet. There had to be war . . .

Var was the chosen one. Half man, half animal, a mutant victim of the blast, he would have continued to live as a savage if Sos had not rescued him from the badlands. And now Var was called upon to repay that debt, to risk his life as the champion of the Empire in a duel he was secretly afraid of winning . . .

0 552 09736 5 40p

NEQ THE SWORD BY PIERS ANTHONY

NEQ THE SWORD is the third book in the trilogy.

An age of darkness was descending upon the Empire. Soon there would be no food, no weapons and no honour – the laws of the nomads were forgotten in the struggle to survive.

Neq was the greatest of warriors. No man faced his sword without feeling its sting. Yet even he could not save the Empire alone, he needed the help of those who had begun its destruction . . . the great leaders who had thought only of war. And so Neq travelled many dangerous miles to find them, knowing that upon his journey rested the future of the world . . .

0 552 09824 8 40p